a Mass for Arras

ANDRZEJ SZCZYPIORSKI

TRANSLATED FROM THE POLISH
BY RICHARD LOURIE

GROVE PRESS

New York

Grove Press
841 Broadway
New York, New York 10003-4793

Published in Canada by General Publishing Company, Ltd.

Library of Congress Cataloging-in-Publication Data
Szczypiorski, Andrzej.
[Msza za miasto Arras. English]
A mass for Arras / Andrzej Szczypiorski;
translated from the Polish by Richard Lourie.— 1st ed.
I. Title.
PG7178.Z3M7913   1993
891.8′537—dc20
92-40176 CIP

ISBN 0-8021-3402-5 (pbk.)

Manufactured in the United States of America

Designed by Ed Kaplin

First English-Language Edition 1993
First Paperback Edition 1994

1   3   5   7   9   10   8   6   4   2

a Mass for Arras

In the spring of 1458, the town of Arras was visited by the disasters of plague and hunger. In the course of a month, nearly a fifth of the citizens lost their lives.

For reasons that remain unclear, the famous Vauderie d'Arras took place in October of 1461. Jews and witches were subjected to cruel persecution; there were trials for supposed heresies, as well as an outbreak of looting and crime. It was three weeks before calm returned.

At one point thereafter, David, the bishop of Utrecht and bastard son of Prince Philip the Good of Burgundy, annulled all the trials for witchcraft and gave his blessing to Arras.

It is these events that form the background to this tale.

HAT night he came to me and said I did not love our town. He even began shouting passionate accusations from the doorway. I received him with the respect due to our teachers and showed him into the house, indicating a comfortable place for him to sit, thinking that the peaceful surroundings and the drink I intended to serve him would cool his anger. But he wouldn't be seated. In the lamp's flickering glow, I could see that his face was very swollen. I had never before seen him in such a fury and would have sworn him mad, but his words attested that he was in his right mind. He accused me of having intended to abandon the town the night before, of which plan he had been secretly informed. At first, I thought to ridicule these reproaches, but, after all, I knew the man. He wouldn't have come to me without proof in hand. The previous evening I had intended to visit David. In total secrecy I had made ready to travel. I left my house before midnight, having sent a man with a saddled horse in advance to Saint Aegidus' Gate. And I found him there at the appointed place. He was shivering with cold and fear. It was a chilly night, with gusts of wind that shook leaves from the trees. To my great amazement, I noticed that the gate was wide open, and the bridge had not been raised. The guards were playing a game of dice nearby. Engrossed in their game, they seemed not to pay the slightest attention to what was happening. I smelled a trap. The minutes passed, filled with menace. My horse pawed the ground impatiently. The moon rose, huge and white as a snowball. Suddenly, I heard footsteps and, a second later, caught sight of a Cistercian monk, who was clearly approaching the town's gates. One of the guards raised his head, glanced without interest at the man, and returned to his game. The monk passed through the gates and stepped onto the bridge. The sound of his staff rang hollow in the dark. No one stopped him, and he walked out of the city. I waited a few moments before returning home where, upon my arrival, I ordered the horse brought back to the stable.

In the name of the Father, and of the Son, and of the Holy Ghost. Amen. Once again the town had played a diabolical trick on me. To leave Arras through wide-open gates would have been immoral! After all, my intentions were honorable, for I had decided to inform David of everything that was happening in Arras. Convinced that the town had succumbed to madness, I desired to spare it further suffering by summoning David, the one person whose wisdom and common sense would put an end to the devilry that possessed one and all. I had thought this idea would meet with resistance from the citizens of Arras. Everyone knew that I had condemned the council's decisions; and it appeared that the council would not stop at expelling me from the community but would take more severe measures as well. I had not closed my eyes during the last few nights. Arrests usually took place after the sun had gone down. When darkness fell, I would pray ardently that fate would spare me suffering. While enduring this bitter anticipation, I returned to the salutary thought that was probably Arras's secret desire as well: David's arrival in Arras would save all the remaining citizens who had succumbed to the madness. Of course, I was aware of the risk involved in this undertaking, but I was ready for anything. Since I had considered the possibility that I might be seized in flight, I had chosen my best horse and confided my plans to a person I trusted. Yet, I then found the gates enticingly open, and the guards seemingly indifferent.

You would be wrong to think that I desired martyrdom and withdrew despite the ease of flight. I was constrained by the council's barbaric faith in my loyalty! If I had doubted the town's madness before, after that night's excursion to Saint Aegidus' Gate, I no longer had any illusions whatsoever.

When Albert appeared at my house late the next day, I was well aware that his was the only mind that could have conceived a plan as cunning as leaving the town's gates wide open.

There was not a wiser or more worthy person in Arras. I grew up in his shadow or, rather, in his glow. The mind of that holy old man had illuminated the path my life had taken. I had come to Arras when very young, still a student, with no knowledge of Scripture, my manners unpolished. At twenty, I was placed in his care and essentially could do nothing on my own, except dully say my prayers by rote. He was quite cordial to me, affording me not only his care, but also that affectionate attachment that a mature and experienced man sometimes feels for a raw youth whom he views as an extension of his own ambitions. I swear to the living God that he saw me as his successor!

I really had no such inclinations. Ghent had made me somewhat capricious, and although my memory of the past was beginning to fade with time, the desire for license and independence remained with me. The people of Ghent take life quite lightly, and as one of the wealthy young people of that town, I often yielded to less than seemly distractions. I shunned neither the pleasures of love nor those of table, nor even those amusements that might strike the pious as blasphemy. But that's not the point here. My time in Ghent convinced me that though I might not truly be master of my fate, I should still always strive to be so. Chastell, who was my protector at the time and enjoyed the favor of the bishop, liked to say that nothing was more wicked than the belief that man is not free. It was usually beside a groaning table that Chastell would say that doubting man's freedom forces you to think with your ass instead of your head. "And then the ass seems made of glass. And a man will think of nothing but how to protect his fragile and so very delicate rear end." Usually, he would add, "In fact, God gave us an ass so we'd have somewhere to be kicked!" This coarseness did not indicate any shallowness on his part. I grew up amid sumptu-

ous feasts, in the company of beautiful women and
noblemen of wit, and came to believe that I was enti-
tled to think as I saw fit.

And so indeed I left Ghent as a youth, with the
swaggering confidence that I was discerning enough
to find my own way. But, truly, when I found myself
alone, without the company of revelers and friends,
without Chastell and the power of his protection, I
soon fell into despair. My first few weeks in Arras
were spent in prayer, fasting, and humility. Soon after
arriving there, I experienced a profound shock in conversation with Albert. He asked me a question that
seemed simple enough, but which had never before
crossed my mind: "What makes you so certain that
you should place more trust in your own mind than in
revelation? Do you believe in God?" I replied ardently
and with all my might that I believed in God. Then he
asked if I believed in the devil. I replied that I believed
in the devil. Then he asked if I believed that God and
the devil fought for my soul. I answered that I believed it ardently. His voice still gentle and somehow
joyful, he asked if I believed that both God and the
devil could influence my thoughts. I replied there was
no doubt of that.

He said, "And thus, the progress of your mind
seems to result from a constant struggle—Heaven's
grace grapples with the promptings of Hell. Where do
you find confirmation that your halting mind, shack-
led by a thousand conditions, influences, tastes, lust-
ful fantasies, fears, and caprices could be clearer and
more able in its knowledge of God's intentions than

the teachings of the Church? We live in cruel times, my dear Jan. People no longer desire to be honorable Christians. They follow the example of licentious princes and foolish bishops, and yield to bizarre heresies. They seek the presence of God in daily life and try to detect God's designs so as to meet them halfway, but God does not want people to strive so zealously for salvation. It is obvious that everyone desires eternal happiness, but they must surrender their fate into the hands of our Lord Jesus Christ and not try to take His place. . . . Jan, trust me! I have spent my life among books and the treatises of the wisest authors. It's laughable! I despise all those usurpers who would save the Holy Church with their belief in reason. The Church's greatest power lies in the sacraments, for they are the narrow footbridge thrown over life's abysses and along which God draws near to us. By remaining faithful to the sacraments, you remain faithful to God. He is with you then, and you with Him. If God gave you a mind, it was not to be used to strive for Heaven but to move about this earth."

When I asked where the soul was located, he touched my chest and replied that the soul was there, the breath of God, the force that allows me to move, to feel scorching heat and cold, to sleep, eat, speak, and think. I asked if it was also because of that force that I desired women. He replied that it must be, for God does not in the least demand that we suffer. God is generous and loves me, and for that reason created woman, so that I might desire and possess her. He spoke angrily: "Only fools think that woman is Satan's

vessel. Woman has an immortal soul and an alluring
body. Had the devil created her, she would have been
toadlike."

Then I was emboldened to ask him if the soul
that I could feel beating in my breast was also given
to all living creatures. He replied that it did not seem
an error to think that dogs, cats, cows, and even don-
keys have been endowed by God with something like
a divine spark that allows them to exist, feel pain and
joy. I sensed in this an unvarnished heresy, and I said
that his words did not seem to me in accord with the
teachings of the Church.

He smiled benignly. "My dear Jan, not everything God desires is found in books, and not everything God intends is known to man, even if he be one
of the princes of the Church. For example, imagine
that your horses and herds grazing in the meadows of
Brabant have some animal heaven of their own.
What's wrong with that? How does that offend Christian teaching? Saint Francis called the horse 'my
brother the horse' and the spider 'my brother the
spider.' Cannot one suppose that the Creator in His
boundless grace and goodness sends down different
fates to horses, cows, goats, and larks, so that they
may know joy and suffering? All that is certain is that
God created man in His image and likeness, and gave
him a mind as well, which has made us the most
unfortunate creature under the sun. What God demands of man is a thousand times greater than what
He asks of a rat, but that does not mean in the least
that the rat is damned for all time. When praying for

yourself and for me, you should devote some of your ardor to the animals, the trees, and the stars, so that they too be entered in the Book of Heaven."

He spoke long and so nobly that tears streamed down my face and my heart overflowed with gratitude and admiration. However, this does not mean that I accepted his teachings without reservation or doubt. My head was indeed empty, but I still had some antic spirit of Ghent in my bones, which inclined me to a certain contrariness. We talked the night away until the sun peered out from behind the hills and lit the back streets of the town. I asked him whether men were equal in the sight of God and in earthly life.

"What makes you better than the man who tends your flocks?" replied Albert. "You are better than he by birth, of course. You were born into good family, called on by Heaven to be a shining example of virtue and justice. Simple people lead simple lives. They should not be expected to perform the deeds to which you were predestined. But this means only that you bear greater burdens. You do not possess herds of fat cows and good horses so that you may wallow in sordid filth, but so that you may be put to sterner tests. When the Lord wishes to afflict a beggar, He sends plague down on him. And when He wishes to afflict you, He also sends down plague. Picture the sufferings of a beggar cowering by a church door, his body covered with abscesses, and picture the sufferings of a rich man, dying in the stifling decay of sumptuous chambers, surrounded by servants, worthy retainers, and beautiful mistresses. You were given high birth only so you could fall from the heights. It is God's will that all the ease and refinement of your existence serves only to make dying harder and sadder. To part with poverty is no difficult thing."

In truth, I had the urge to scoff at this teaching, for I had no taste for such verbal flourish. I was disgusted by Albert's skillful habits of thought and by his loquacity that sprang from olden times when people were unable to speak of anything but God and His Saints. Oh, I was zealous in belief and a pious Christian, but I did not wish to spend my entire life tracking God's intentions and interventions in order to please Him. What God wished to make of me was His affair. And I thought mine was to live in accord with my nature, as it was bestowed upon me. Think me a drone, if you wish! Indeed, I had but a single desire—freedom! If God stood in my way, I would go around Him. And I hope that in His boundless goodness He will generously forgive me.

Freedom.... In the name of the Father, and of the Son, and of the Holy Ghost. Amen. Freedom means to be as Heaven created us. Free to be foolish and wise, to be licentious and to suffer, to be happy and unhappy. For all the respect I harbored for Albert, I always saw a bit of the obtuse cleric in him. Oh, how he longed to fight for the salvation of souls. Animated by his mission, he even honored mayflies. But I also saw this mission as a threat to my liberty. When he took pleasure in the mantle of prophet and teacher, he was no doubt free, but when he tried to force that cloak onto my back, he became a tyrant.

Once he assigned me to dispute a commentary by the venerable Jan Gerson, which took three long weeks of work. It was springtime, and the town was bathed in sunlight. Just before New Year's Day, Prince Philip had come to Arras with a brilliant and merry court. As you know, there were a good many Englishmen about at the time, for even though the prince was playing them false, they still remained on his estate, drinking and carousing at Burgundy's expense. There are always Englishmen wherever good times are to be had. When the thaw came, Philip left for Brussels, but a variety of people stayed in Arras, gluttons, loudmouths, rakes, and a few women of easy virtue as well. This did not surprise me. Philip was aging badly, becoming ever more vehement in prayer, and was loath to look upon that loud, lewd rabble. And so a portion of his court thought it prudent to remain in Arras under David's rule, which was lenient and remote. Royal bastards are more lenient toward sin than their nobly born fathers. And so that spring Arras was thronged with a boisterous bunch of Burgundians and Englishmen, all fond of drink. Among them was an English wench, well versed in the arts of love. I was twenty years old and dreamed of her at night. I threw Gerson's commentary to the floor, and many times after took that wench wandering through the meadows and had my pleasure with her. One day Albert attacked me and struck me in the face. I suffered terribly from the pain and humiliation, and by the time I had recovered, the wench was no longer in Arras.

Albert called me in to be examined. I spoke haughtily: "Where is the certainty that it is worthier to worship God with a disputation on the work of Master Gerson than with the loins? You have spoken to me of love, Albert. I love the belly of woman a hundred times more than books by dotards from the Sorbonne. My glosses don't mean a thing to Gerson! He's turned to dust, and at best we'll see him in the Valley of Jehoshaphat in five thousand years. And as for the English girl, we tasted happiness together in the fields outside the city, but where is the certainty that this displeased God?"

"You're blaspheming!" cried Albert.

It was always the same. When he preached, wisdom and tolerance poured from him like water from a spring. But if one tried to live according to his precepts, Albert would immediately threaten him with hellfire. Inwardly, he cultivated a pure idea—that there existed a marvelous harmony between God and man—but he was sickened by any attempt to make it manifest.

In the name of the Father, and of the Son, and of the Holy Ghost. Amen. Everything seemed fine, gentlemen, but really it was Hell. Picture my life at the side of that worthy and intelligent man who might be held an exemplar of all virtue. He would say to me: "Love the animals for they are your younger brothers." But when a hard winter came and I ordered my horses given good grain, he reproached me for reckless squandering.

He would say to me, "Love woman, for she is

given you by God." But when I kept a mistress in the house, he threw her out, yelling loud enough for the whole town to hear, and accused me of debauchery, which, needless to say, evoked mirth throughout Arras, where every self-respecting townsman had more wenches than saddle mounts. He would tell me, "Love those near and dear to you, and treat them as equals, for they are your equals." But when I tried to follow that teaching, he would flog me, shouting that I was descending into madness. He told me not to abominate Jews, but he would not eat in my house because Jewish bankers from Utrecht had eaten there. And, what's worse, there wasn't a drop of hypocrisy in him. He would walk about the city of Arras in the armor of his faith, so modest he was almost haughty, so wise he was almost foolish, so good he was almost base. There was only one thing on earth he feared more than Hell, and that, gentlemen, was David!

I was present at one of their conversations. David had suddenly arrived in Arras with a small retinue. He came to see Albert and, when greeting him, bowed low to the ground. David was tall, black haired, tanned by the winds of the north. Albert, on the other hand, was stooped with age, with a long gray beard, and skin white as snow. The royal bastard —an indefatigable rogue, the devil incarnate, a glutton, a liar, full of wild pride and the most madcap ideas—faced a wise man composed of knowledge, gravitas, and virtue. Two forces, like dogs freed from

their chains. Oh, I tell you, that was an excellent conversation.

Albert invited David to dine with him, to which
David cried in reply, "Your Honor, gnawing on roots
is not my idea of supper!" He always called Albert
"Your Honor."

Albert flushed scarlet and muttered softly, "Oh,
my prince. . . ." Needless to say, the feast was everything it was expected to be. David ate as much as ten
men, tossing bones everywhere, sucking grease off
his thumbs as he thrust them deep in his mouth. I
kept a close eye on Albert, who seemed to have suddenly lost all appetite. I swear I could see what Prince
David was doing! He was not at all as roughhewn and
boorish as he wished to appear at that moment. He
whinnied like a horse and farted noxiously at the
table, which did not make a good impression even on
those wholeheartedly devoted to him. He really over-
did it a bit. But only when they started to converse
did the bishop of Utrecht begin to shine.

They spoke of the nature of man. As usual, Albert
clung to two charitable formulations: "Prince, whoever truly loves his own mother and is gentle with
animals, as Saint Francis taught and enjoined, must
without fail be a good person."

"But of course!" roared David. "I had a rowdy in
my employ who would strangle the occasional unruly
subject for me, slip poison into drinks, or jab a knife
in someone's ribs on my orders. One day, he came to
see me in tears. 'What happened?' I asked the knave.

'Prince, my mother died today at daybreak,' he said. He was so inconsolable that, imagine this, Your Honor, for a few weeks I had to free him from all work because his hand was shaking so, that he might have crippled someone instead of dispatching him to Heaven. And, as for animals, he loved them warmly, tenderly."

Albert shot him a furtive glance, bit his lips, and said that the exception only proves the rule. David replied that he too was an exception because he loved his mother greatly, cherished his horses and hounds like few others, but probably did not enjoy the reputation as the best man in Brabant.

"Your Majesty is just being capricious!" cried Albert.

For nearly half the night I was doubled up with laughter at their arguments. With a good-natured smile, David explained his purpose in coming. "Your Honor, I have come to Arras because I have received reports that the citizens are weary and dejected from constant fasting, processions, and other efforts to win eternal salvation. I too am concerned with their salvation. I swear by Christ's holy wounds that I think of nothing else, and nothing causes me such affliction as the decline in morality. But the thing is the poll tax in Brabant is drying up, and my royal father is extremely exasperated that the income from the northern cities is so meager. Commerce here is like a wind-broken mare, the walls of the cities are crumbling—no one has so much as touched them since the time of the English oppression—the high roads are so full of robbers and wandering penitents that there's no room for the merchants. I would be glad to take the welfare of the town of Arras to heart, but don't forget, Your Honor, that we must eat our daily bread. The soul is the soul, but the body must have its crumb too."

"Your Majesty!" cried Albert.

The bishop cut him off with a gesture of his hand and went on talking, his tone less good-natured now. "You and I work hand in glove, good Father. Go on saving souls, Your Honor, but in two Sundays' time you will pay my tax collectors sixty ducats."

Albert's hands were trembling. "That great a sum!" he cried in despair.

"If I scratched a little harder, I'd find thousands in your coffers," said David.

"I cannot do that," said Albert. "I will not pillage the people of Arras."

The bishop burst into such laughter that he nearly fell off his bench. After a moment, he spoke: "Father, where is it written that people are more eager for salvation than for worldly riches? The town of Arras is dying! Life is bad here and becomes harder all the time. You preach to the people constantly about God and His Saints, and you give them the Sacrament, but in the meantime, cattle are eaten by mange, houses are falling down, people have no clothes on their backs and nothing to put in their mouths. People are fleeing to other parts of the duchy where there is less sanctity but more food. I will put this town on a new footing with the sixty ducats I receive. You know me, Your Honor, and you know I am a good husbandsman. You think that when you impose hardship on people with God's Word on your lips, it's easier for them. I do it differently. If I have to squeeze people, I do, and if I must relent, I relent. There are many laughing faces to be seen in Utrecht, but in Arras all lips are tight in prayer."

Albert rose from the table and lifted one hand. Then I knew that he was about to utter one of those marvelous pieties of his with which he had been plying Arras for twenty years. "Your Majesty, above all we must love those we govern."

David bellowed with laughter again. "To hell with you, Albert! They don't give a damn for your love! They don't care about being loved; they care about their own well-being! What does it matter if you love them, if things go ill for them? Very few people love me in Utrecht, and I love no one. But I want to see satisfied faces and all bellies full, for only then will I feel safe to enjoy life!"

"Your Majesty curries favor with the crowd," exclaimed Albert. "If they desired pagan spectacles, you would not refuse them! You thirst for applause, whereas, more than anything, I seek to elevate the hearts of men."

"Go to hell with all that elevation of yours, Albert. Had my father observed all your precepts, I would never have come into the world. He sired me in sin. I am the fruit of his misdeed, but I know that I was conceived in pleasure that a proper union would not have afforded my father. And so, Your Honor, do not demand elevated feelings of me! I am closer to the people of Arras, who need bread and amusement, than you are, Father, with your sermons."

"Every ruler who struggles to save the souls of those he rules is a man alone," said Albert.

"Empty talk, Your Honor. Not every ruler, but only he who wishes it."

Just then Chastell, who was attending the bishop, leaned toward him and said softly, "Come what may in Arras, you must admit the good Father is pure as the driven snow!"

"And what if he is pure, if he's a fool!" snapped the bishop of Utrecht. Indeed the man's words could hit the mark. Who else could strike at Albert's heart with such telling accuracy?

It all began innocently, as it were. Who would have thought that such a trifle could lead to such dreadful events? A horse died. It had belonged to a clothier, Gervais, known as the Damascene because years ago he had spent time in Syria and had extensive connections with the merchants there. Truly, it was a singular occurrence! Especially since the horse was strong and healthy. A two-year-old of good blood, used for riding and given special care in its owner's stables. As I was saying, the horse was healthy the previous evening. And when the master made the rounds of the household before going to bed, he had noticed that the horse was in fine form, and ordered the groom to saddle the mount in the morning and bring him to the gate, since Gervais wished to accompany a shipment of serge as far as Lille. The next morning the groom crept into the master's bedroom and said that the horse had died. The entire household flocked to the stables. The horse lay motionless on the earthen floor, its belly distended, foam clotting its nostrils. "What did he eat last night!" cried Gervais. He was told that the horse had not been given anything. "My horse has been poisoned!" shouted the clothier. This was not at all possible, for the building's gates had been closed before nightfall, and all the household retainers had been there for years and enjoyed their master's confidence. Gervais was to lament the loss of his beautiful saddle horse for quite some time.

Around noon that day, he was visited by an acquaintance, a ropemaker, a wealthy man who kept three servants and owned a stretch of orchard outside town. The ropemaker said, "Damascene, I hear you've suffered a great loss: your horse died last night. . . . You should know that I was passing by your stables and by torchlight saw a Jew by the name of Tselus. I heard him hurling curses at your entire household."

The ropemaker had hit the mark, for the Damascene had had a quarrel with Tselus for years. And indeed the powers of darkness must have had some hand in the horse's death, for who had ever heard of an animal dying so suddenly? The Damascene hastened to the town council and lodged a complaint. I was not present, having other business that would brook no delay, but I do know that it was Albert himself who heard the clothier. "Provide a witness," he told the angry plaintiff. A moment later the rope-maker was presented to the council. "Will you swear to what you have seen?" asked Albert.

"I swear by Christ's wounds."

Farias de Saxe, who was learned in the law's jurisdiction and regulations, and sat on the council for want of anything more interesting to do, said to Albert, "Father, you should not attempt to examine a matter concerning townsmen. Even if today they are satisfied with your verdict, tomorrow they'll raise a cry that you're using the town to carry out your own will. It would be better for them to hear Tselus themselves."

There arose a dispute of no little significance. Albert, who had never renounced the pleasure of meting out justice, objected to Farias de Saxe's views by citing Tselus's religion. "Where is it written that municipal courts should try a Jew? Anyone can sit in judgment on a Jew!"

Farias de Saxe replied, "And where is it written that anyone can sit in judgment on a Jew?" Albert of course won the argument because the result was truly important to him, while everything was an amusement to de Saxe. He was too rich and bored to attach importance to anything. Once when I came upon him in church by the confessional, he told me that he sinned out of boredom and confessed out of boredom as well. He really was the only great lord in the town of Arras! May he rest in peace.

And so Tselus was brought before Albert. "Did you cast a curse on Gervais' house?" asked Albert.

"I would not be capable of it, Your Honor."

"They say that you are a wise Jew."

"All the more reason why I would not be capable of it!"

"Does that mean that an effective curse requires ignorance?"

"It means that for some, and something else for others. Everyone hears what he wants to hear!"

"Admit it, Tselus, you hate Gervais the Damascene."

"Am I obliged to love him, Your Honor? If I am, then I will love him."

"This is not the first time you've come before this council, Tselus. Three years ago you desecrated Christian corpses."

"Your Honor is in error. I had nothing to do with that. I was not in town at the time, as the investigation proved conclusively."

"Yet you do not deny that you were implicated in that affair."

"I cannot deny that, because it was so. . . . Yet . . ."

"Tselus, we have received reports that you refused lodging to Count de Saxe, as custom enjoins."

"Your Honor, Monsieur de Saxe will testify that I have always welcomed him with proper humility. Monsieur de Saxe has stayed, along with two greyhounds and one pointer, and I never denied him his rights."

"But you don't consider those rights to be fair?"

"It is not for me to pass judgment on what is fair and not fair in the town of Arras."

"Should that be taken to mean that you find the city alien?"

"That's not what I said, Your Honor."

"But it's what you think, Tselus."

"With all due respect, how does Your Honor know what I think?"

"You are not here to ask questions but to answer them."

And so it went until late in the night. I felt sorry for Tselus even though he was a Jew, but I did not intervene. The ropemaker's statement had been accepted as proof, as was obvious from the start. That night Tselus hanged himself in the cellar of the town hall. Monsieur de Saxe had the audacity to announce to Albert, "Father, the blood of that Jew is on your conscience."

Albert replied loftily, "You are speaking of what you neither know nor possess."

As Farias de Saxe left the council hall, he muttered to me, "People like him are always the worst. They kill in innocence." I heard that Monsieur de Saxe drank fiercely that day. It must have been one of the few days in his life when he was not bored.

But it was not Farias's drunkenness that caused anxiety in the town. In the name of the Father, and of the Son, and of the Holy Ghost. Amen. Gentlemen! Today your view of the citizens of Arras may be marked by ill will or perhaps even outright loathing, for indeed they did commit acts whose like the world had never seen before. But such was fate. I knew those people. They were not evil—they were certainly no worse than the other burghers of Brabant or the duchy as a whole. Surely, Arras had not produced very many saintly men and virtuous women. There was much envy, baseness, and swinishness there, and many a scoundrel had built himself a comfortable nest within the walls of the town; but that evening when news spread of the death of the Jew Tselus, nearly every citizen admitted complicity in his death. Oh, I shall not attempt to prove here that they loved the Jews and the red patches on their cloaks, or that it was without distaste that they rubbed shoulders with Jews on crowded market days, or that they trusted the word of a Jew. Every citizen understood that the Jews were an alien element and that God was sorely trying the townspeople by condemning them to live alongside the killers of Jesus Christ. But it was precisely because they were true Christians and submitted to the will of Heaven that their town became a soil in which the Jewish seed could grow.

I enjoyed no sympathy in Arras, that is certain! I was a newcomer from another land, eye and ear for the court of Utrecht, and so people gave my house a wide berth, for they did not trust me. Still, they came to me that evening with tears and lamentation. "The Jew Tselus hanged himself in the town hall!" they cried in horror. "Albert did not treat him justly. Woe to us, for God does not forgive such infamous sins."

"What should I do?" I asked.

"Go to Bishop David, who is your friend, and ask him to come to the loyal town of Arras. Without him here, misfortune shall befall us all. We desire to wash away the innocent blood that has fallen on the citizens of Arras. Let the bishop tell us what we should do."

What was I to answer them? It seemed laughable for me to travel to Utrecht or Ghent, to stand before David and request that he go to Arras. From my house, I gazed down on that disconsolate band of citizens, and imagined David's smile as I presented that request from his flock.

Gentlemen, you know the bishop better than I. He is a great man and an exemplary Christian. And yet, I imagined myself arriving in Ghent, my horse left dead on the road. Covered with dust and sweat, my face battered by the autumn wind, I enter the bishop's chamber. David greets me fondly: "Glory to the Most High, you're here, Jan! I'm off to a hunt tomorrow—you'll accompany me."

"Your Majesty," I say. "I am here as an emissary from the town of Arras. Its people humbly request that you go there, for they fear God's punishment. Albert drove a man to his death, a Jew by the name of Tselus."

"A Jew, you say!" replies David with a smile. "And I'm supposed to go rushing to Arras on account of a single Jew?"

"Not on his account, Your Majesty, but for the people of that ill-fated town!"

"And what am I to advise a town that is suffering

from hiccups? I would never think to dispute with Albert over some dead Jew. God has given, and God has taken away! And you, Jan, stop worrying. I've got a wench of great beauty from Speyer. I'll give her to you for two nights."

I say in despair, "Your Majesty, the people of Arras are overwrought. I fear disturbances. My lord, you know how easy it is to inflame passions in these times of hardship. The wounds from the terrible cannibalism of the past have not healed yet. The town has scarcely emerged from the flood, and now once again . . ."

David brings his hand to his face as if driving away a bothersome fly. I fall silent. Then he says, "Pax, pax! What was the story with the Jew?"

"A person testified that the Jew Tselus had cast a curse on the house of a clothier whose horse of good blood had died. The horse was healthy and was to be ridden the next day when suddenly, in the middle of the night, it fell dead in the stable on account of the Jew's curse."

"What color was it?" David asks and laughs.

"That I do not know, My lord."

"If it was bay, I don't feel sorry for it."

"My lord! I'm telling the truth. The town is troubled."

"You tire me, Jan. If they're in the mood for penance, let them flagellate themselves. Tell the people of Arras that the bishop has ordered a procession and a ten-day fast. But in his own way that Father Albert vexes me greatly. His accounts are simple—one horse, one Jew. But I have to reckon with God. What am I to say to Him? How am I to know if in God's estimate the Jew should have been killed? Maybe one Jew, maybe two, maybe only half a Jew. . . . I don't know what a horse is worth in the stables of Heaven."

My going to Ghent would have amounted to very little. And therefore I told the people to return home and see what tomorrow brought. And I myself went to speak with Albert. He received me dryly as he usually does when anticipating a quarrel. He had never overcome his belief that though I was his pupil, I was still an outsider, someone who belonged to the immense world beyond the walls of Arras. Even after many years — although I had given him ample proof of my loyalty and almost filial devotion — he would still chide me for some affinity with David and, even worse, with Chastell, whom he hated with all his heart. How many times did he reproach me for a lack of Christian zeal, attributing it to the pernicious influence of Ghent. And how many times did he bitterly repeat, "My dear Jan, to you it seems that reason must be admired above all else. And you think that your protectors from Ghent, David chief among them, hold reason in the greatest reverence. Meanwhile, despite appearances, what is of importance here is not reason but the genitals. David exercises his faculties in bed. He thinks he is strong because he believes in nothing. How stupid that is, Jan!" Without saying it outright, he always suspected that I was closer to the bishop's court than was in fact the case. He thought that David lent an ear to my advice. Meanwhile, David saw in me a friend and companion in dissipation but always sedulously avoided serious conversation with me. But Albert was not mistaken in thinking that in my heart I had more of Ghent than Arras. And I found that a bit flattering.

And so, this time I was somewhat constrained with Albert. The very fact that the townspeople had turned to me requesting that I intercede at the bishop's court made me feel awkward. And I was not surprised in the least when Albert, having listened to my account, remarked gruffly, "If they sent you to David, why have you come to me?"

I spoke in the gentlest tones I could elicit from my throat: "Father, it isn't proper for the bishop's court to involve itself in local disputes. The townspeople are upset because of incidents that have taken place within the confines of the town, and therefore the proper decisions must be made within those same confines."

He glowered at me, then shrugged his shoulders with reluctance and irritation as if wishing to shed some burden. "That does indeed sound wise, but on your lips, Jan, it smacks of hypocrisy! Is the death of that Jew going to bring you in accord with this town as you never were before? Mysterious are the ways of God. Suddenly, at this dangerous moment, when there is occasion for David to intervene in our affairs, and when the townspeople, always so vigilant that no one breach their privileges or violate their rights, are of their own free will soliciting a decision by the bishop's court, you become the guardian of the town's freedom and shudder at outside interference in the affairs of Arras! When at last a dispute arising between myself and the citizens has provided David with an excellent opportunity to make me a laughing-stock, to mock and humiliate me in the eyes of people whom I have always loved, you choose to show me forbearance, Jan! Watch that David does not hold you accountable for that faintness of heart!" Then he fell silent and drew closer to me. He looked me in the eye with an expression of both watchful suspicion and what seemed admiration. "But do you understand?" he asked suddenly, seizing my hand. "Be sincere, Jan! Have you understood what's taking place here?"

I swear to God, I had no idea at the time what he was driving at. He must have seen that in my eyes, for he broke into a derisive laugh. "Well, all right . . . how could anything like that even enter your mind!" He had probably never held me in such disdain as at that moment when he perceived that he had overesti-mated me. And he at once became imperious, aloof, even free of the mockery which, given his nature, cold as ice, lent him at times a bit of inward warmth.

He spoke: "Remember that you were a mere pup when you came to Arras years ago! You owe your success to this town. It made you an educated and wealthy man; it bestowed its confidence on you and endowed you with some power. . . ." I interrupted: "Father, you deserve the credit for everything you ascribe to the town of Arras!"

"What's that?" he replied. "You're well aware that there is no boundary separating me from the town and the town from me. I am the town, the town is me. If I did something for you, you should be grateful to all the citizens of Arras, for they exercised power through me. For years now, I've been telling you over and again that anyone who contests me, speaks against the town, or attempts to violate the laws and privileges of this place becomes my enemy. It would be laughable were my path to diverge from that of the citizenry in this hour of trial. Only despair and confusion of mind could have caused them to come to you with a request to summon David. I have plowed this soil for twenty years and have transformed that soil. The people here do not love the bishop! And he has done nothing to deserve their love. Whenever he comes here, it feels as if the town has been beset by a gang of plunderers. We live as honest men in Arras, without the luxury and iniquity that consume Utrecht and Ghent. What has happened to Brabant, where now there is universal hypocrisy, intrigue, contention, and depravity? David maintains hired brigands at his beck and call to settle accounts with those who oppose his court. Have you ever seen any outlaws in Arras? Does our town need to employ dagger and poison to kill its enemies under cover of night? We have achieved a unity here that seems blessed by God and by the people."

I said, "Father, the Jew Tselus hanged himself in the town hall!"

"I'm aware of that. . . . The poor Jew! God apparently wished to make a sacrifice of him. Remember, Jan, nothing has happened that could encumber

our town. The town council had not passed any sentence, yet. Tselus took his own life of his own free
will. Can't you see how people are here, how dis-
tressed and pained they are by the death of that unfortunate man? Picture something similar happening
in Ghent or Utrecht. The very idea is laughable! Who
there would care about one dead Jew? Whereas the
people here desire purification. And they are receiv-
ing purification! And thus I want you to understand
how iniquitous and foolish are all attempts to appeal
to David's reason. You must not only display gratitude to the town of Arras but show accord in its
times of trouble."

"That's just what I thought," I said calmly. "And
that is why I have come to you, Father, though the
citizens demanded I travel to Ghent."

Then Albert broke into harsh laughter again and
said, "Jan, I've known you for many years. And I have
never doubted your loyalty. Go back to the people
and tell them that it would be dishonorable to seek
support at the bishop's court. We alone are masters
of Arras, and the fate of the town lies solely in our
hands."

"Would it not be more suitable, Father, for you to
inform the town of this yourself?"

"No, my dear pupil! I have never concealed from
the citizens the feelings that I harbor for David. And
for that reason my decision could be ascribed to ill
will and mistrust on my part. Did they not come to
you with their request for intercession? Who would
be a better emissary from the town of Arras to the

court of Utrecht? It would be a good and judicious thing were you to explain why you are refusing the mission entrusted to you."

"You are right, Father!" I said.

In the name of the Father, and of the Son, and of the Holy Ghost. Amen. Gentlemen! I only feel partially guilty for what God sent down on the town of Arras. I was His instrument, and I trusted in His justice. But allow me now to call the recent past as my witness: those terrible days three years ago when our town was stricken by plague and hunger. I think that it is there that one must search for the reasons that I acknowledged Albert's arguments as correct.

Cattle had begun dying in the spring of that year. At first nothing in this seemed out of the ordinary. After a severe winter, a number of cattle always grow thin, lose their appetites, and die without cause. However, as you recall, that winter more than a few shepherds also commended their souls to God. We had walked out of the town in a procession to the ringing of the bells. The cold, rainy days had come, but then suddenly the sky cleared, the sun shone warmly, and hordes of vermin began to appear within the walls of Arras. The vermin crept into the town from meadows that had been soaked and then had suddenly dried. Nothing of the sort had ever taken place before. The town was surrounded by clouds of vapor: in the morning and at nightfall you could not see a person an arm's length away. The sun was very hot during the day, but the walls rang with cold at night. People began dying. First one, then two, then ten. Their bodies decomposed with tremendous speed, becoming black and swollen. Those who performed the last rites could not breathe because of the stench. Almost immediately fires began breaking out, consuming much property, especially the stores of provisions laid up against lean times. It was then that Prince David journeyed to Arras. Welcoming him at the gates, I told him, among other things, that few rulers would display such courage as his. In time of plague the eminent usually flee to the first place they think of, leaving all they own for the mob to plunder. Times like these offer the best proof of how little worldly goods mean when God sends mortal peril down. David thus displayed rare fortitude and compassion by coming to an Arras in the grip of plague. He rode through the town gates with his grand retinue, preceded by a man carrying a reliquary with a drop of Saint Aegidus's blood, a gift to the bishops of Utrecht from the counts of Saint Gilles.

However, his arrival, which gave heart to all the townspeople, soon brought hardship. David introduced a strict regime. I do not in the least maintain that he intended to ruin Arras, though this was thought by many. Under threat of capital punishment, all food touched by the hands of people who had died of the plague was to be burned. When the madness of this course was pointed out to him—what goal could be served by stripping the town of its meager remaining reserves—he replied that he placed his trust in the advice of the doctors at his court. By that time he had already surrounded himself with the pack of hangers-on and braggarts who trailed him across the length and breadth of Brabant and poisoned his great mind with nonsense. Worse still, when departing from Arras after those days of harsh discipline, he ordered the gates closed and a watch set up along the walls.

"You're dooming us to extermination!" cried the members of the town council.

"Pray then!" he replied.

Truly, he did not abandon us in our need. Each day copiously laden wagons drew up to the gates of Arras. Every morning the creaking of wheels and the cries of drivers were heard. The townspeople would gather on the walls as the bishop's envoys unloaded the wagons. When they drove off, cracking their whips and whispering prayers, the bishop's guards would allow us to open the gates and bring the food into the town. It was divided fairly, much to the credit of Monsieur de Saxe, a man of great rectitude and unbending character. Still the plague continued to reap its harvest, and signs of hunger were ever more apparent in all the people of Arras.

Then came the days of desperation. Having learned of our misfortune, nearly all of Brabant's marauders, armed bands devoid of conscience, pressed upon the town. Lying in wait in the wooded hills, they would ambush the bishop's wagons by night and loot them. David increased the guard, but this produced no results. The lure of easy booty fired the imagination of scoundrels throughout the duchy. Making no secret of their intentions, they came from its most distant corners to line their purses outside the walls of the dying city. Once the thievery went on for three days before our very eyes, for we could see everything from the heights of the walls. David paid the wagoneers in gold and precious stones, but daredevils willing to risk death could no longer be found. Hunger assumed terrible proportions here in Arras. Guards were posted in the cemetery, for there were even those who, abandoning shame and Christianity, would force open fresh graves and feast amidst the stench of corpses. Rumors reached us that a woman had squeezed the life from her newborn child, cooked it in salted water, then ate it, feeding the remaining broth to her other children. When brought before the council, she admitted to the deed. That was the day when the town's anger toward David was at its height. The citizens cursed his decision. "David has buried us alive!" was the cry that went up around the town hall. Some demanded severe punishment to be inflicted on that degenerate mother, but others were of the opinion that the guilt for that act fell upon the bishop. I admit without fear that I shared that view.

We put the woman on trial. "She must be made to suffer!" cried the citizens to Albert.

After a long silence, he said, "I will not cause her to suffer. Let God be her judge."

So it was decided that the woman was to be beheaded the next day at dawn, even though the town demanded that she be consigned to torture. An enormous crowd gathered in the marketplace. In that hungry throng only the woman condemned to death had eaten her fill. Sword in hand, the headsman climbed onto the platform while soldiers dragged the woman there. She was praying, full of humility, reconciled to her fate. We waited for the ritual of justice to commence. Albert said not a word. His head held high, he was staring at the sky. That was a bit strange. Time passed. The executioner hung back, glancing impatiently at Albert. The crowd began to mutter; some excitement had seized every heart.

"What are you waiting for, Father?" someone suddenly shouted from the crowd. "Grant her absolution!"

Albert said nothing. He was still staring at the sky as if looking for a sign.

I drew close to him and said softly, "Father, time to begin."

"Let them begin!" he muttered.

I could see one of his eyelids twitching, a sign of anger in him.

"What!" I exclaimed. "But you know you must grant her absolution for her final journey."

"No," said Albert. "Give the executioner the sign to cut off her head."

"Father," I cried, "I will not do that! The sentence shouldn't be carried out without the viaticum!"

"I have been generous to that woman," said Albert. "The people wanted her burned in fire and tarred . . . so cruel of them! At the trial I said explicitly that she would not suffer, and that God would determine the poor woman's fate. Order the executioner to perform his duty."

We spoke in whispers, but the people standing near us got wind of our disagreement. There was an air of dread about the crowd. Cries broke out, then weeping. People fell to their knees around the scaffold, and they all raised their voices in prayer, calling to Albert to show Christian pity for the unfortunate woman.

It took her a short while to understand what was happening. "Father!" she cried out in the greatest of despair. "Have pity on me! Let me be burned alive, torn apart by horses, but do not refuse me that final consolation. It is true I have done wrong but do not take such a cruel revenge."

Farias de Saxe walked over to Albert and seized him by the arm. "Don't defy God, old man!" he shouted in fury. "Give that poor woman the viaticum if you hold your life dear."

Albert glanced at de Saxe as if he were a worm crawling underfoot. "Teach me no lessons about virtue and sin, Count, for you are not worthy to instruct me. And don't dangle death before my eyes, for I do not fear it. One more word from you, and I will order the soldiers to seize you and hang you from a dry branch."

De Saxe bit his lips, then said more calmly, "Father Albert, you are usurping a right that belongs to God. Without absolution, that poor woman must spend eternity in Hell!"

"Must she?" said Albert with a mocking smile. "Why must she? Do you think that I have concluded a compact with God that makes Him afraid to repeal my decisions? Who do you think God is, de Saxe? He's no merchant of Ghent, you fool! By His will alone shall that woman be hurled into Hell or sit at His side among the angels. You miserable worm, do you think that I have a contract with God, or that He can be haggled with?"

De Saxe whispered, "Father, do not refuse that woman. . . ."

"Stop whining, you fool! You're all alike. The whole crowd's the same! So that's it! Do you all think that if I refuse her the viaticum, she will be condemned to eternal damnation?"

"Father," I said calmly though I was choked with rage and alarm, for I felt I was brushing against something murky and fathomless. "The priesthood has given you the right to act in the name of God. God has entrusted a portion of His will to you, and consequently it is in His name that you dispense absolution."

Albert laughed quietly, his gray beard quivering on his chest. "Fools!" he snarled. "It is true that I serve God, but where is it written that a master should be loyal to his servants? In your heads you imagine that by taking one decision or another I thereby tie God's hands! But God is omnipotent and omniscient. A thousand years ago He decided all that is happening here today. Leave me, Jan, and you too,

Count de Saxe! Let the executioner cut off the woman's head."

What was I to do? I walked over to the headsman and said to him, "Do your duty."

He cast a wary glance at me. Through the slits in his hood, I could glimpse the anxious flash of his eye. "It's a sin!" he muttered.

"It's not for you to pass judgment," I replied firmly.

The woman's head rolled. The huge crowd wept, and some people said that God would punish the town of Arras for such a cruel deed. After this event the town's mood changed. David was no longer cursed, but Albert. David even displayed magnanimity to the town when later, by virtue of his authority as bishop, he absolved the woman who had been put to death and delivered her from Hell.

I remember the night when Albert learned of the bishop's decision. "Now there's David for you!" he cried. "God's closest friend! I can see already what's going on in Heaven. God is being advised that the bishop of Utrecht has absolved that woman of her sins. A great flurry in the chambers of Heaven, much ado, and worry. The Lord is disconsolate. 'I had done everything so well,' He says to Himself. 'And then an oversight like this. Now the bishop of Utrecht might be displeased. Take that woman from Hell as soon as possible and transfer her to the fires of Purgatory.' And this is carried out by messenger angels, one of whom races to Ghent to humbly report that it has been done as the bishop had deigned to decide. Then what? The angel has to wait because His Majesty is busy, with feasting or harlotry. Fools, fools, fools! They imagine that God is their confidant or their confederate or their support in contention! But have they ever seen Him? Have they ever spoken with Him?"

"Father Albert," I said at the time. "There exist certain principles that form our life and lead to our salvation. It is within the bishop's power to act in the name of God, and although the nature of that covenant is difficult to discern, one still must believe that Heaven expects men of the cloth to make decisions in accord with the teachings of the Church. . . ."

"The teachings of the Church come in part from God and in part are the work of men," interrupted Albert.

"Father, I agree . . . but it is well to remember that without special grace the revelations of the Church could not have become law."

"That is another matter," grumbled Albert. "And I do not wish to share with you my thoughts on that subject."

Truly, he spoke like a heretic. But, even so, he was one of those who had been granted the privilege of brushing against heresy. He communed too closely with God for some doubts not to have grown within him.

I will now return to the thread of my story. And so plague raged in the town. The gates had been bolted fast from the outside and anyone planning to escape into the world made an easy target for the bishop's guards. The citizens were very agitated. They felt their desolation and misfortune so keenly that they were disappointed in those whom they had trusted for so long a time. Prince David had surrounded them with an impenetrable cordon, and although he tried to relieve the town with deliveries of food, the bands of robbers doomed his good intentions. Albert, on the other hand, had betrayed the town by refusing an act of Christian compassion and forgiveness to the unfortunate infanticide. Thus did the citizens of Arras see themselves as having reached the lowest depths. They began to revolt and blaspheme, having concluded that God Himself was mocking them.

A hundred years earlier, such sentiments would no doubt have been impossible, for people were extremely pious and compliant to the dictates of Heaven. But nowadays? More and more we hear that our earth is round like an apple, and that it does not stand still at all. It is also said that the human body has a host of similarities to the bodies of dogs, cats, and even swine. Knowledge of every description disturbs the mind deeply, and doubt steals into no few souls. The world is undergoing a change whose bounds are fluid and unfixed. Would it even have been thinkable a hundred years ago for people to gather in cemeteries and perform astounding yet reverent rituals in worship of death? In our forefathers' time death was death, and no one was astonished by the obvious fact that our bodies decay, then dry out, finally to turn to dust. Yet today people are stirred to their depths by this, and all Christian hearts are filled with dread in the face of death. There is a certain despair in this, a certain wavering, as if our minds had conceived the thought that everything ends with our final breath, that in dying we enter nothingness, darkness, a nonbeing where even the knowledge of that all-embracing void does not exist, and thus even that void does not exist . . . there is nothing, there is nothing. . . . In the name of the Father, and of the Son, and of the Holy Ghost. Amen. What can a human being encounter that is worse than the harrowing thought that God is infinite darkness? To liberate themselves from that thought the flagellants stream out onto the roads, inflicting suffering on themselves, flowing with blood, and beseeching God to become their light and life. Our piety is gaudy and gloomy, not like that of Saint Francis, who taught people how the sun, the flowers, and the breeze should be enjoyed. Today, who experiences joy from looking up at the sky and seeing the splendid flash of a star or the shape of a cloud? Who finds pleasure in the colors of a flowering meadow? And, finally, who touches the bark of a tree and feels a pleasant quiver from communing with the handiwork of God? In air musty from hissing torches, amidst fumes from censers, in the presence of the Almighty, who watches over altars, we beat our foreheads against the stone floors of our temples. We shriek out our sins in the belief that naming our acts will liberate us from their burden. I may be gravely mistaken, but I think that we are coming to the end. The hour in which the world shall perish is not far off. God will absorb us all into Himself so that He may continue to exist in the solitude of His own being. And indeed this is a frightening thought though it ought to bring joy to every Christian heart.

As I have said, the town of Arras was suffering. That unfortunate woman, executed by order of the council, was not the only criminal at that time—such crimes had multiplied. People had ceased to fear Hell and all its extravagant tortures, and wanted only to satisfy their hunger. Man's animal nature now gained the upper hand. Graves were dug up, and the dead subjected to terrible cannibalism. There were cases in which families finished off the dying so as to have fresh meat free from the reek of putrefaction. As might have been expected, when people foresaw the end of everything, the most unbridled license seized the town. Women of exemplary virtue behaved like harlots. One could observe scenes of indescribable lewdness played out in broad daylight, even by the church gates. Mere language cannot express how odious and heinous it all was. When the daughter of one nobleman fell ill, he burst into tears and laughter, then threw himself upon her crying that it was not right that she leave this world without having tasted the pleasures of the flesh with a man. "God would not be that cruel to my child."

The town was undergoing an ordeal, but the worst of it was the knowledge that no help could be expected from any quarter. People felt that they had been buried alive, left utterly to their own powers and devices. Truly, it was that feeling which freed them from the bonds the world usually imposes. Soon they felt so isolated, so abandoned by the authorities, secular and spiritual, so utterly doomed, that they began to think that everything that had previously bound them to the world was now devoid of value. In that hour of terrible ordeal, decimated by plague and by hunger, they felt as if they were on a deserted island, surrounded on all sides by a meaningless, indifferent, and impassable sea. But these feelings were not the only thing acting on their imagination. At first, in the face of misfortune, nearly everyone became equal and the time-hallowed rights of the privileged lay in ruins. Artisans, lords and priests, men and women, old people and children, all died in like manner. Entering the town's gates on his black horse, Death knocked at all doors, paying no heed to the station of the household. Abominable rats swarmed through the town under the scorching sky and, with indiscriminate appetite, attacked the bodies of the dead, whether the flesh be aristocratic or plebeian. Farias de Saxe, whose pride seemed stronger than his desire to live, kept careful watch that every mouth in Arras was equally fed its scanty portion.

At first this singular equality prevailed, though not devoid of savagery and madness. Someone incited a crowd, which then followed him to the Dominican monastery where learned books had been collected for centuries. Without cause, the crowd made an enormous stack of the parchments and set them on fire. As flames shot up, people took each other's arms and began dancing in the glare of the fire, amid clouds of smoke, until late into the night. They destroyed everything not fit to eat. A time of new values ensued, and—I daresay—it seemed that despite all the suffering and bitterness, people were breathing more freely! Suddenly, nearly everyone felt that his previous life had been encumbered with a multitude of unnecessary whims and delusions. People did not say, "What do we need books and learning for now?" but, "What good are books and learning at all if, against our will, our time passes, and we must leave this world without having known joy or delight, or even true unhappiness?" Having come to doubt the fundamentals, they soon began to doubt in God as well. With every passing day, God grew less needed, for He was not present. He had departed from Arras, consigning it to plunder by its starving citizens. Then suddenly our bodies—dying, emaciated from starvation, inflamed by plague—assumed the greatest significance. People looked with tenderness on their own faces, arms, stomachs. Nothing but the body was of value, and nothing more deserving of affection. It so happened that those who were fatter than others experienced special pleasure and were shown a respect bordering reverence. But that did not last long, for it was precisely those saddled with fat who were the first to fall to the knife. Knocked off their pedestals, they ended up on one table or another. Then began the tyranny of the thin and sinewy. A dreadful terror broke out, and the savagery mounted to its climax.

Human nature is ridiculous. When the woman who had murdered her child was tried, everyone thought Arras had hit the very bottom of misfortune and affliction. Later, people would recall the trial as evidence of idyllic days, long gone. A town in which trials are held, laws applied, and verdicts passed is not a town forsaken by God. There was no longer anything divine in Arras, where it was later calculated that every third person had perished from plague or hunger. We had been left alone with our humanity, our bodies, and imaginations animated only by our stomachs.

It was a rather cruel liberation. All people, no matter what their station, had always been part of an all-powerful hierarchy. It cannot be denied that hierarchy is a blessing, but it also cannot be denied that it is a leash and collar. Oh, I do not think that someone born a peasant suffers because of what he is or desires to be something else. Only a very narrow mind could conceive such an illusion. It seems obvious—a peasant is a peasant, and thus everything about him is peasantish, every particle of his body. He would have to stand outside himself and his way of life in order to perceive his own peasantness as I perceive it. And the same is true of me! Everything about me is lordly. I breathe like a lord, in keeping with my destiny on this earth. I don't know how an artisan thinks, for I am not one, and if I were able to make conjectures about his way of thinking, they would still be a lord's conjectures. Hence, I do not claim that in those terrible days of hunger and plague the peasants felt themselves our equals. At first the peasants looked to the lords for protection and rescue. When the peasants realized that even the highest born were powerless, they knew they were lost. But the powerlessness of those above them, which at first cast them into despair and despondency, later became a source of a certain strange strength for them. Since the protection of the mighty was unable to meet the needs of the moment, it lost all its value. In becoming orphaned, the peasants became self-reliant. Similarly, the lords who looked to the town council and the Church for help realized that they had been abandoned by the council and the Church. Throughout his life each of us had submitted to those above him, but when hunger and plague suddenly toppled the ladder of hierarchy into the dung of universal powerlessness, each of us, without exception, discovered that he was separate from the world. We were orphaned and condemned to death, but we were no longer subject to anything except ourselves. A terrible solitude had overtaken us, but there was something sublime about it as well. Hitherto, in living and in dying, all of us, without exception, had been in a state of subjection; and I do not doubt that this state can be full of sweetness and may give us a sense of security. Yet in that state, we make efforts to please others, those above us and those below. Submission is the beauty of our existence. And, in exchange, we receive protection and peace; in a word, it allows us to enjoy life. Without it, fate leaves each of us prey to himself. And so it was that in the hour of agony, a mixture of terrible anguish, despair, and lasciviousness, the citizens of Arras whispered to themselves, "I am the son of man. I am the son of man and nothing more!" This unbearable burden lay heavily upon us, most likely causing our descent to the lowest depths.

But our minds were working well, as well as possible for people suffering the cruelties of hunger. Some people experienced revelations and conducted conversations with their patron saints in Heaven. Skeptical lords, accustomed to subtle reflection on the nature of man, could be observed chatting with invisible beings as they strolled the streets of Arras. In conducting those conversations the lords maintained the most courtly manners, smiling and bowing to their interlocutor who had arrived straight from Heaven. There was no mystical exaltation from fever or disease in any of this. These people remained themselves in every word and gesture, but someone else had emerged from within, a life companion hitherto confined and silent, who now, in that most terrible hour, had become their equal, allowed to accompany them as they headed toward their death. It also so happened that monks who had spent long years in prayer, fasting, and penance crawled out into the sun from their gloomy monastic cells, gave themselves over to licentiousness with women, and loudly blasphemed God. But what might seem most strange was that every person in Arras had in reserve some sensible explanation for his own metamorphosis. I think that reason had never before known such brilliant triumphs as in those days when values were everywhere in decline. People were able to find a justification for every sublimity and misdeed. It was characteristic that the precision of those justifications made some people more equal and others less. And that returned some sense of measure to our life in Arras. It became evident that it was impossible to live without some standards of value, to live only for the stomach, in the stomach, by the stomach. That was a powerful standard, to be sure, but still not an entirely satisfying one. That everyone without exception wanted to eat did not mean that everyone was equally evil, good, noble, or base. And so a new hierarchy began to appear in the town among the emaciated, desperate specters. Some people became teachers; others were their pupils. And it did not seem important in the least what constituted the substance of those lessons; what mattered was the very fact of a new set of superiors and inferiors, new ties that allowed people more easily to bear the burden of annihilation.

It was scarcely three years ago that all this happened, so how can one be astonished at what the people of Arras did in the fall of last year?

When it seemed that all was lost and there was

no hope for us, the plague suddenly ended, as if God had recognized that we were living in Hell! At first people did not realize that fate had taken a different turn. From one day to the next fewer and fewer people died; and, in a surfeit of good fortune, the armed bands withdrew, and once again each morning we could hear the creaking wheels of the bishop's wagons laden with provisions. It was like a dream. We did not even realize that we were getting enough to eat and returning to health. Scenes of blasphemy and lewdness continued, but slowly the passions cooled, and with that an indescribable shame sprang up in Arras. Those who had disputed with their patron saints now scoffed at Heaven, while those who had threatened God now flagellated themselves before church gates. Farias de Saxe no longer apportioned the food, for now there was plenty for everyone. And once again the common folk had to make do with food of lesser quality, while the lords demanded the best. And, as in the past, no one objected. Slowly, equilibrium returned, albeit fragile and weak, for certain experiences had taken root in people's memories; and although everyone gave humble thanks for being spared, they could not take joy in life as they once had. Seeking refuge in hierarchy and community, people retained their sense of isolation. For some, shame was harder to bear than plague. Even though an air of forgiveness enveloped the town, and people pretended that nothing had happened to sully their honor, still nights were uneasy in Arras, full of bad dreams, desperate memories, and humiliating tears.

By then Arras desired purification and sought a formula to explain the crisis that it had lived through.

On the day when the town gates were opened, all the bells pealed triumphantly, and an enormous procession encircled the town's walls. Toward evening a heavy rain began to fall, which washed away the last traces of our crimes. The next morning, under blue sky, lit by an early sun, Prince David rode into town. He was greeted with the humility due a revered pastor who is the son of the king, but without the love usually heaped at the feet of a benefactor. When, accompanied by Father Albert, David blessed the throng, a goodly portion of the citizens of Arras bowed their heads without bending their knees.

Albert said softly, "Forgive them, Your Majesty, but they have been sorely tried by fate and have despaired somewhat."

David replied, "What do I care about their faith and their despair? What matters is that they survived."

To tell the truth, I felt somewhat affronted. If someone does not appreciate our despair, he appreciates neither us nor our lives. But I held my tongue, for I did not think it seemly to make objection to the prince.

The atmosphere was strained during his visit, which does not mean in the least that the prince had changed his attitude toward the town, or that the town harbored any deep sense of grievance toward him. The body's satiety soon causes a calming of the spirit, and few now recalled that it was on the bishop's orders that the town had been cut off from the world. What had happened was that the paths of our experience had diverged somewhat. While we had consorted with plague and hunger within the walls of Arras, David had feasted in Ghent. I would not wish to be too frivolous on this point. No one doubted the prince's sincerity or his desire to come to our aid, but it is one thing to rescue and another to be rescued. One thing to suffer and another to have compassion for those who suffer. And, finally, it is one thing to know of something and another to know the thing itself. The prince knew that death exists, while we knew Death itself. Having emerged from the abyss, we experienced a kind of nostalgia for the experience that had been vouchsafed us and had enriched us. No one in Arras recalled the days of plague aloud, but they were thought of frequently, as if they contained some source of strength, a secret impossible to disclose and entrusted to us alone, the people of Arras.

No doubt, this was the reason that the bishop's whims were not received with the indulgence they had once been shown. He took this as a sign of a grudge on our part and was somewhat angered by it. When he gave a feast, the citizens of Arras ate little and drank even less, whereas the bishop's court, as always, indulged themselves immoderately.

David leaned toward me and said, "I can see that my food sticks in people's craws. What's all this sulking about, Jan? Watch out, or I may take this as an insult from them."

"Prince, do not judge us too harshly," I said. "We love you as before, and it is a joy for us to feast at your table; but our taste is different now. Every mouthful of meat causes us sensations of which the Brabant palette has no idea. Food came to mean survival for us, and none too sweet a survival at that. What once brought us joy is now but mere necessity. We are not to blame for that, Prince."

"Arras was always inclined to exaggerate," replied David. "It's a town with exquisite scholastic traditions where once there were disputes over the number of hairs in Beelzebub's tail. I do not doubt that you have been through cruel suffering, but where is it written that this is cause for glory?"

"We don't desire glory, Your Eminence, but calm, safety, and peace. We do not boast of our suffering. I even think that when we recall those recent days, we feel more shame than boastfulness. What's important is that it now belongs inalienably to us. Arras cannot renounce that suffering, it cannot relinquish it, it cannot eradicate it. It has become a part of us. Have I made myself sufficiently clear?"

"You've made yourself clear, but that doesn't change the complexion of things: namely, knowingly or unknowingly the town of Arras is forcing me to participate in its sufferings. It sticks its wounds and cemeteries in my face when I want to enjoy life and provide amusement. Perhaps the days of hunger and plague have ennobled you greatly, but there is no reason that your suffering should become an example for others. The plague afflicted Arras, but it did not afflict Ghent. Does that give you the right to claim you are better?"

"We don't feel that way, Your Eminence."

"On the contrary," he said very sharply and struck the table with his hand. "On the contrary, you do, and you show it by emphasizing your difference, by putting it down to your bitter afflictions. No one under the sun emphasizes his difference to humble himself, only to elevate himself. But since you are sitting here at my table and I am your host, I wish that my appetite be yours, my amusement be yours, and my small-mindedness be yours."

"Who would dare impute any small-mindedness to Your Eminence?" I cried in amazement.

"Everyone here," he replied, making a circle with his hand to indicate the revelers. He said this very loudly and many heard him.

I cannot believe it now, but I did feel shame at that moment. I was not ashamed for the prince but for Arras! After all, right was on David's side. Not on account of what he had said, but because he was David. He was born to be right. And at that moment the entire table understood that the world was returning to its time-hallowed course. The salutary state of his divine right put an end to our despondency. After a moment of silence, cries rang out as they usually do at feasts, and shortly everyone was given over to wild pleasure. Only Albert remained gloomy. Sitting to David's right, he leaned toward him

† 56 †

and said, "Prince, how cruel is your hatred for this town."

David replied, "I hate suffering, dear Father."

To which Albert responded, "Today, that comes to the same thing, Prince!"

David said, "You've hit the mark. . . . Let it be as you say! I do hate Arras!" And he burst into merry laughter as if finally free of something.

In the name of the Father, and of the Son, and of the Holy Ghost. Amen. I don't believe that David was telling the truth when he said that. Rather, he was expressing his antipathy for Father Albert and used words that would injure him. It is quite impossible that so great a lord could hate one of his towns and all its inhabitants. I do not deny that we irritated David by our bitterness and the depths of the suffering we had endured. One way or the other, we were the most sorely afflicted of all the inhabitants of Brabant, which could have aroused anxiety in the bishop's mind—we might wish to exalt ourselves over others and might even reach for the heights where he resided. If so, David was greatly mistaken. In fact it was during this feast that all the citizens of Arras concluded that it was good to have a father, a shepherd, and ruler in this man who was so strong, firm, and full of the joy of life. Oh, how we did like him then. Late that night, when people had become somewhat drowsy, the bishop summoned the court players to the banquet hall: singers, poets, and also a clown, very bawdy and amusing. When they came in,

David asked them, "What shall you perform for us, my dear friends?"

"What would you like, Your Majesty?" they replied.

David said, "You know me. I make no demands. Decide freely as is always done at my court."

And so they sang and played what pleased them. I then said to the bishop, "Your Majesty is very kind to them. It's different here. Father Albert keeps a tight rein on that sort."

David burst into joyful laughter. "I support artists because I am not afraid of them. I don't demand anything of them. They're completely free with me."

"I think they must be glad of it," I replied.

"Nothing of the sort!" cried David. "It fills them with fear, Jan. They are not sure of the day or the hour. They don't know what I have up my sleeve and constantly suspect I am up to some trick."

"But that's childish," I said. "Their prince does not conspire against them."

He said nothing and looked at me with a touch of mockery. A moment later he said, "Let's drink, Jan."

A dozen or so people sitting near us had heard what he said. A shudder went through me, but the others seemed to take heart. They craved his power and cunning. They wanted to consign themselves to the protection of a person who could guarantee their safety. They realized that a ruler who had secrets of his own was worthy of their confidence. They had long since doubted Albert. His prayers and sermons had not turned misfortune away. He had demanded that Arras place its faith in Heaven, but Heaven had remained indifferent in the face of plague and hunger. And so people were prepared to trust David who, to be sure, had not promised to absolve their sins but had been sufficiently stern and powerful, sufficiently cunning and cold to put an end to their afflictions. To a certain extent, the people of Arras had been afraid that David would seize it by the throat, but what was there to fear now that they had eaten their fill and the gates of the town were open?

I think it is here that one must seek the reason why the citizens came to me when the Jew Tselus hanged himself. Three years had already passed since the terrible days of hunger and plague, but the memories were still alive in us and the hope was still strong in us that in time of need only David could save the town. In truth, the bishop had scarcely visited Arras twice, and had spent these days feasting, amusing himself, and hunting. Yet his very presence caused Arras to feel more secure. After the days of plague, life swiftly returned to its old routines. Once again Albert taught humility and purity, once again he encouraged fasting and strict morals, once again he argued that we are the chosen sheep of the Lord's flock. Now he conducted trials with leniency and justice as if fearing to incur God's wrath, which he had undoubtedly done when he refused the viaticum to the unfortunate woman who had murdered her child. Truly, Albert had been aged and saddened by that affliction. In accordance with David's wish, Albert moved the cemetery outside the town's walls. The bishop of Utrecht had written him: "Do not keep places of eternal rest in the very midst of the town, for that will not save the dead but poison the living. Leave your dead in peace. Do not traffic in them, as you have done before, in order to further ensnare the living in your teachings of eternal salvation. The dead have already rid themselves of you, good Father. They sleep soundly in their graves, dancing with the worms; and the Lord God has embraced their souls, and He is in charge of them. . . . Have people buried outside the town walls. This I expressly command you once and for all. . . ."

So much did we learn from the bishop concerning municipal affairs. Yet everyone thought that an appeal to the court at a difficult moment would find safety there, a shield. That is why the people had come to me and clamored that I make haste to the bishop's court and report the great injustice done the Jew Tselus.

But I did not go! I went back to them and, in accordance with Albert's wish, told them the following: "I have considered the matter. I spent the whole night thinking of what I should do. I prayed fervently in hope of God's help. You have come to me troubled because of the apparent transgression Albert has committed. And that is testimony to your Christianity. Still, I thought to myself that your goodness has a lining of pride. After all, there is no question that the Jew Tselus cast a curse on Gervais' house. What else can explain the sudden death of a healthy horse? But, for the sake of a clear conscience, the council decided to conduct a thorough investigation. So, no sentence was passed on Tselus, no one uttered the word 'Guilty!' Had the accusation proved a fabrication, the ropemaker would have been held accountable. Meanwhile, Tselus was held in the town hall, as is customary. Where then is the impropriety?"

One of the townsmen interrupted me, calling out, "Tselus was not granted the right to a defense!"

"He had yet to be tried," I said. "That was a preliminary hearing, and he responded to the council's questions. Had the time for a trial come, he would certainly have been allowed to defend himself according to law and custom. But he eluded the trial and the town by taking his own life. And, in so doing, he gave proof of his guilt. Does an innocent person take refuge from justice in death? He was so sure that his guilt would be established that he carried out the punishment himself."

Then someone said, "Or maybe he had no confidence in the justice of Arras and wished to spare himself suffering?"

And another cried, "That can't be. After all, he condemned himself to eternal damnation!"

And yet another called out, "He was a lousy Jew all his life, and that itself was enough to damn him. Since his fears weren't our fears, don't say that he believed himself condemned to eternal damnation. When the Jew Tselus hanged himself in the town hall, that was not the way into Hell for him, but the way out of it and into something promised him by his Jewish faith. And so it cannot be claimed that he punished himself. Perhaps he was only seeking peace."

The person who said this was a staid and well-dressed man. He looked like a jurist but was in fact de Saxe's steward, to whom the count had given some rich lands years ago, and who had made a great fortune from them. I will speak of him again. At the time I asked him, "So you think that Tselus had no confidence in the justice of Arras?"

"I didn't say that," he replied with a wary look in his eyes. "Perhaps he only feared suffering and because he was a weak person, devoid of Christian faith, he left this world of his own will."

"Was he guilty in your opinion?"

"I was not his judge, sir," he answered haughtily. "Nor would I have wished to be. Since uncertainty always weighs on me, I always admit the possibility of error, and for that reason I keep to one side. Besides, we did not come here to argue whether the Jew Tselus was guilty or not, but to request you to be our envoy to Prince David. He is our ruler and we trust in his wisdom."

"So I see!" I spoke sharply. "But just think for a moment. Why would you summon the bishop to Arras? The Jew Tselus lies dead in the cellar of the town hall. You cannot resurrect him, and, even if you could, it would most likely not be pleasing to God. If the bishop is to come to Arras, he must be told the reason for the journey. On whose behalf is he to come, and against whom is to he act? No matter how

we pose the question, the bishop would have to conduct a trial—on one side the dead Jew and on the
other the town of Arras. If right is on the side of the
town, why annoy the bishop with a long and burden-
some journey? And if right is on the side of the Jew,
then woe unto us! One man here spoke sensibly when
he said that he felt uncertainty and admitted the possibility of error. However, while you can encumber
yourself with that burden, you cannot take it from the
bishop's shoulders. The bishop is, like all of us, only
a human being. Do you think that God always speaks
through the bishop's lips? One might have thought
this a hundred or two hundred years ago, when the
world was ignorant and yet more exalted than it is
today. We are aware of our defects. I am among the
bishop's friends, which is a source of honor and joy to
me. But I tell you frankly, for I hold truth dearer than
all, that the bishop should not be summoned. We are
not the favored sheep of his flock. Moreover, we enjoy
privileges, and to infringe on them would be a grievous sin. The town of Arras has its own council, its own
courts, and its own justice. To rely on Prince David
means not only to consign ourselves to his protection, but to surrender to him those rights that constitute our wealth. Even if we are not just, we are unjust
by our own standards and on our own account. You
say that David must be trusted. That is true. And who
doesn't trust him? Are there any such people in this
town? But trust in Prince David cannot cancel the
trust we place in ourselves. It could be said that
David's idea of justice is like David himself. God is

always like the man who believes in Him. For, as you know, God is our longing for truth, for love, for the sublime. God is the better part of us, and belief in Him is the road to perfection. But the better part of me is one thing, and the better part of someone else is another. Each man has his own measure. . . ."

They listened to me with a certain astonishment, even a hint of alarm. I myself was aware of the blasphemous tone that I took but kept speaking, confident that, acting in the service of a good cause and with a definite aim in mind, I could count on Heaven's favor.

I continued: "When are we close to God? When our conscience is clear. In truth, the ignorance of sin will open the gates of Heaven, even to sinners. If I do evil but think I do good, then I am doing good. If I do good but think I do evil, then I sin. God's Church teaches us what is good and what is evil, and shows us the way to salvation. But God Himself is something we bear in our hearts. And I tell you no one knows my God, and I know no other God apart from my own. I am who I am because I have my own God who is not the God of other people. Though He is at the same time the One God and the Almighty. . . . So what is it you want? For the bishop to impose his suppositions and views, his conscience and justice on our town? And for the town of Arras not to stand by its own conscience? Does God not visit our hearts, and do we not try to commune with Him in our own way, meaning the way that pleases Him? We are as God made us. And it pleases God that Arras is the way it is, not better, not worse, not wiser, not more foolish. . . . Our life is a mystery. It forms an Ark of the Covenant between us and God. What do we need a strange god for? Strange gods are needed only so that we can express negation. For everything we do is negation. Each of us denies who he is. To be yourself means constantly to cry out that you are not someone else. Truly, were the bishop to travel here, the only way to affirm our identity would be to not submit to him! Then what is the source of our conviction that the bishop's faith and justice are better than our faith and justice? And even if they are better, they are not ours! And since they are not ours, they cannot determine our faith and justice. They turn into their own contradiction; they become despair and wickedness. If David comes here and conducts the trial, Arras will lose itself. Upon returning to Ghent, the bishop will take with him everything that constitutes our existence. We, on the other hand, will remain caught in a net of indecision, wrongdoing, and evil, though some persist in the illusion that they have been improved by the bishop's rectitude and faith. I tell you again, anyone who divests himself of his rights and surrenders his faith to others, entrusting them to seek God, that person renounces salvation. . . ."

They listened to me with anxiety and uncertainty. I myself was frightened that I was going too far. But I had sown despair in them, for when I finished, the man who was de Saxe's steward said, "Well, there are some things I hadn't thought about yet. I think that what we've heard here is very interesting. Indeed, the bishop could draw too far-reaching conclusions from our request. Meanwhile, we probably have enough rectitude to deal with our fate here, within our own walls, without outsiders, though they be as august as our lord, the bishop of Utrecht. As for the case itself, it is plain enough. No words can bring Tselus back to life, but still we must look into all the details. Albert did not act as he should have, and he ought to give us an accounting of himself. We harbor respect and love for Albert, but if the bishop cannot stand in our stead, neither does Albert have that privilege. Then let the case be turned over to the town, so that we may decide whether the Jew Tselus was guilty of a crime."

When the steward concluded, the majority was in agreement with him. There were, however, those who left in ill temper, thinking I had merely outtalked them.

That day saw the beginning of an unusually democratic administration in Arras. Certain there was no longer any danger of the bishop coming, Albert willingly allowed the plebeians to take part in the council. The others approved this new arrangement without anger, but not without a hint of raillery. De Saxe said to me that evening, "Look how Jewish blood unites good Christians. Nothing better to bind this town. The only pity's that the council chamber now stinks of manure and raw wool."

On the other hand, Albert announced with a dignity and a strength of conviction, which surprised even me, that it was in Burgundy's best traditions to pay close heed to the common folk, and there was nothing unusual in this. From this day on, he proclaimed, citizens of all estates would sit on the council, for that was how it was back when Prince Jean spilled the blood of the Armagnacs to please the poor.

This had a beautiful ring to it. The citizens of the town bowed low to Albert when they were before him. Only de Saxe muttered, "Something stinks here, but the stink is so dignified and paternalistic that I must think a highborn ass has befouled the air."

In the name of the Father, and of the Son, and of the Holy Ghost. Amen. From that day on, strange things began happening in Arras. I do not at all maintain that this should be ascribed to any initiative on the part of the local carpenters, clothiers, and blacksmiths who sat on the council. All the same, it was their very presence and participation that opened entirely new perspectives. It could be said that what happened in the town was akin to something we at times observe in nature. There can be very gusty winds in autumn in Artois. Some blow deep inland from the sea and are dank through and through. Others roar down from the wooded hills that stretch to Paris and are unusually dry. They collide over the fields of Artois as they roll whistling by. This can cause rain and the sort of foul autumn weather that keeps a mist suspended over the town from dawn till dark, or it can cause clear, mild weather that is rather refreshing. Sometimes the wind from the sea absorbs the other one—and then the town is struck by a downpour, the streets are flooded, and the trees stripped of their last leaves in seconds. It also happens that the very dry wind absorbs the full force of the other, and then, for a few days, scorchingly hot weather prevails, which is very unpleasant at that time of year. The orchards turn yellow from the sun's rays, the vines receive too much heat and have to be given to the cattle as fodder. As long as those two winds battle each other, Artois has a mild if capricious autumn. But if one or the other triumphs, we must pay dearly for that loss of equilibrium.

Something similar happened in Arras when the common folk began sitting on the council. Suddenly, we lost the independent element of the street, which, wisely or foolishly, had in some way moderated the council's resolutions. As far back as my memory can reach, Albert and his closest associates had always treated the citizens of the town the way a man treats a woman he desires to possess: with a touch of contempt, of fear, of tenderness. For twenty long years, Albert was solicitous of what the people of Arras thought. I think that kept his mind in a state of tension and anxiety. The townspeople treated him with a fearful respect, but this did not mean that they bowed their heads humbly and kept their mouths shut. They usually had their own views and made plenty of noise when something important was at stake. Convincing them of anything was hard work; a way had to be found into their coarse minds, which were sometimes narrow and sometimes incredibly quick. It depended on the situation. Years ago they had wanted to side with the English, and it never occurred to them to follow Burgundy's example of joining King Charles. The town flourished under English rule. Even though armed bands engaged in plunder and violence, the citizens of Arras continued to weave their beautiful tapestries and sell them at a profit on the other side of the English Channel. The poverty of the French court was too apparent for the artisans and merchants of Artois to quickly ally themselves with King Charles. In vain did Albert then argue that Jeanne was a good woman whose sword had been blessed by God for use against the English. People took her for a trollop and cursed the day she'd gone to Chinon. A few years had to pass for them to accustom themselves to the new situation. The textiles were then sent to Brussels, where the duke of Burgundy overpaid for every ell of serge, so as to win Arras over to his new policy. But the town, though flourishing again, continued to like the English and dislike the French.

In those years, Albert had performed masterly maneuvers to unite Arras with the cause of the court. And many times he had to think long and hard to strike the right note, for the citizens were jealous of their privileges, knew wheat from chaff, and always kept their own interests in mind. And these two forces were like the opposing winds that grapple over Artois, bringing good to people, animals, and plant life.

But now—everything was changed! Ropemakers and carpenters entered the council to deliberate there. Either the street had swallowed up the Reverend Father, or he had swallowed up the street. There were no longer any conflicting elements. Harmony reigned. That was the first curse Heaven cast on Arras.

Gentlemen! If you think that from here on, the council's sessions became a field of argument and bitter dispute, you would be grossly mistaken. Just consider the situation! Previously, the common people had been informed ex post facto of the council's decisions. Sometimes they barked out against those decisions, crying, "No, no, and once again no! Father Albert, reconsider, for we do not agree and will not act in accordance with your decision. We're telling you, reconsider, so not to anger the town further." Then the council would reconsider the issue, making sure that their new decisions would seem different, milder or more severe, in either case easier for the townspeople to swallow. Yet the street never took part in those decisions. The commoners could cry "No," but protests were futile. This caused Albert great travail, but made a prudent ruler of him. But when the street entered the council, it began to take part in making decisions. But what good was that?

Who is a carpenter in his own home? In his own home a carpenter is lord and master. And who is a carpenter in the street? In the street a carpenter is a citizen. And who is a carpenter on the council? A carpenter on the council is a humble close-mouthed person. Sometimes, when pulling in his net, a fisherman must struggle very hard, for the fish resists, its tail thrashing the surface of the river. The fish is still in its element, the fisherman is not. But just let him drag the net ashore, and everything changes: the fisherman stands firmly on a rock as the thrashing of the fish grows weaker and weaker, until all motion ceases and the fish can be impaled on a spit without any trouble.

And so it was with the common folk on the council. They were out of their element, and, even worse, the ease of opposition had as well been taken from them! No longer could they cry, "No, no, and once again no! Father Albert, we're telling you—no!"

Now, when they wished to cry out, they were told, "You have the right to protest, and we are glad you are making such proud use of it. But first the appropriate decisions must be made, and then you can say what you think of them!"

Thus, an unimagined burden had now fallen upon them. They writhed like caught fish, and at first they again cried out, "No, no, no, we don't agree . . . ," but since they were men of substance and conscience, they fell silent. Sweat ran down the backs of their necks, tears filled their eyes, they looked at each other with despair and fear, saying, in the end, "Let it be as Father Albert has bidden!" What else could they have done? They lacked the swaggering confidence that accompanies the wellborn throughout life. They felt constrained by the subtlety and elegance of the nobles' speech, the grandeur of the chamber, the furnishings, and the garments. Most of all, they felt constrained by their own new sense of responsibility.

Indeed Albert had earned himself eternal salvation, if not by his deeds, then doubtless by his cunning. For he achieved something of which all rulers dream. By ceding a measure of power to the common people, he attained absolute power. By sharing it with fools, he kept it all for himself! This was something even Prince David had not achieved, perhaps because he made light of everything, his own power included.

And a new administration began, one promising to be harmonious. No one supposed that this was the worst burden fate could have placed on the shoulders of Arras. It was astonishing that now when I would encounter commoners, they did not have a single word to say about the case of Tselus. It was as if it had disappeared on its own, slipped into oblivion. I said to Monsieur de Saxe, "How faintly the flame of justice burns in their minds. A short while ago they were crying out in defense of the Jew, and now they seem gagged in the presence of the council's grandeur and ready to barter a clear conscience for the crumbs of importance that fall from our table."

De Saxe replied, "I really don't see anything unusual about that. Why do you expect more determination and obstinacy in matters of conscience from simple people than is encountered among lords? They're just confused, that's all." De Saxe was a man of great delicacy, was he not?

But anyone who thinks that the shadow of the Jew Tselus no longer fell across the council chamber is mistaken. The carpenters and the clothiers said nothing, but Albert at least did not wish to remain silent. And that brought on an avalanche of subsequent events.

A person came to the council bearing a letter from the Jews requesting that they be given Tselus's body. He was shown in. The man stood in the shadows of the low, vaulted chamber, as black as he could be. His clothing was black, his beard was black: I thought of him as a tuft of holly blasted by winds. He remained silent while we read the letter. The town hall's caretaker stood right beside him, a very stalwart and roughhewn man, a head taller than the Jew. At the time I thought that in some odd way this Jew stood above us all, for he knew something we did not yet know: for us it was today, while for him it was tomorrow. Yet, I may not have thought this at the time, feeling only an anxiety and a chill, as if I had been touched by the wing of a bird in flight.

Everyone looked at that dark Jew, but he looked at me alone, the way mutes look at those who can speak, or how intelligent animals look at people. By God, that wasn't easy.

"What's this!" said Albert softly. "Are the Jews now dictating their rights to the Town Council of Arras?"

The Jew bowed his head. "We hold the council in the highest esteem," he said. "And we humbly present our request to the council." He bowed his head even lower.

In the name of the Father, and of the Son, and of the Holy Ghost. Amen. The world is hopelessly constructed. Imagine the existence of an ox. Yoked, it goes among the fields, its head hanging low, in expectation of the whip. It is brought on a tether to be slaughtered, and it bends its knee when it is about to be killed. But what if good luck had made it a bull instead, what then? It would be useless to yoke it, for it would tear free of its tethers and trample any field. It takes five big men to drag a bull to slaughter, and it sometimes happens that the bull breaks their bones, filling the air with its terrible bellowing. An animal's nature changes completely if it has a sense of its own strength. And the same is true of people! Where did the restraint of the good wheelwrights of Arras vanish when they began sitting on the council's benches? The solitary figure of the Jew was met with looks like those of enraged bulls. He did wrong to speak so humbly for, at that moment, nothing was as loathsome to them as humility. Their large noses had caught a savage scent. Had he only hurled haughty words at them! But, no, he stood motionless in a bow that was taken as a gesture of weakness and reverence. For people of Monsieur de Saxe's ilk, and for me as well, who were accustomed to a certain respect, there was nothing unusual about the Jew's deference. But those commoners sitting on the council, on account of Albert, were experiencing such delights for the first time in their life.

One shouted, "Bow your head lower, Jew!" The Jew complied.

I glanced over at Albert. A smile emerged from his fluffy beard. "I do not see in your letter the respect owing to the council," said Albert. "You come to us with a request, but you need to be taught how to bow properly. We are forbearing, but mind that you do not exceed the limits of our patience."

The Jew replied, "Sir, it is not the fault of my fellow Jews that they selected such a base and wretched emissary. If need be, I will accept punishment with genuine respect, but I do request that the Jewish community be spared your wrath, for it is not to blame!"

"What a slippery Jew!" shouted the baker Mehoune, thus causing a general uproar.

But Albert held sway over the rabble. "Pax, pax!" he cried. "Such emotion is unworthy of the council!" They quieted down. Then our Reverend Father asked the Jew his name.

The Jew replied, "Itzak." Albert dismissed him with a gesture of his hand.

"Sir, how can it be that the council leaves a Jew's insult unpunished?" said Mehoune.

"I saw no insult here, baker," replied Albert.

Again they began shouting, but he calmed them down. He spoke to the baker. "Mehoune, do you really think that that Jew knowingly desired to humiliate the council?"

"Yes, I do!" shouted the fool, red with anger and panting for revenge.

"And how about you, Yvonnet the clothier?"

"I think so too," replied Yvonnet.

In turn everyone made the same reply. When Albert was finished with them, he turned to me. "Jan, my dear friend, what do you think?"

"I think," I answered, not without fear, "that the Jew acted boorishly toward the council!"

The Reverend Father smiled gently and said to Monsieur de Saxe, "And you, my dear Count, what do you think?"

De Saxe hissed like a cat. "My dear Albert," he replied, not hiding his fury, "I am a de Saxe. How can I feel offended by a Jew? Me, offended by him?"

Albert said gently, "Everyone knows that the counts de Saxe are the flower of Brabant. Thus it is obvious that a piece of Jewish dung cannot soil your cloak!" After these words were spoken, I felt a wall of cold antipathy and mistrust form around the count.

That would have been the end of the session, but then Albert added, "My Christian conscience whispers to me that poor Tselus is not guilty of what happened here today. And so I request the council to resolve to give over the body to the Jewish community. Let it be buried according to Jewish custom. As for the Jewish community itself, we will return to that question at another point."

It was so resolved. People dispersed to go about their business full of righteous anger. That night they fell asleep moved by a sense of their virtue and prepared to mete out justice to the Jewish community. They felt purer and more honest than they ever had before. By the bedside of each stood the angel of the holy war that had just been declared.

As for me, I remember perfectly that I did not close my eyes at all that night. I was tormented by fears that I would not be able to name today, for an autumn and a good stretch of winter have passed since those events took place. The snow of Flanders has fallen over a portion of my memory, and the winds blowing in from the English Channel have swept all sorts of images from my mind. All I remember is that when the sun rose and it began to grow a little light, I fell into a troubled sleep. I dreamed that I was wandering through some unknown place, entirely deserted and seemingly fashioned from a single immense stone. My steps left no trace on the surface of the earth. I could see no people, no animals, no trees, not even any grass. Just bare, hard stone extending all the way to the horizon, and me alone under a billowy sky. It probably did not last very long, because when I opened my eyes, the sun was still low over the roofs of the town, and night's piercing cold had yet to recede. But even if the dream had been brief and fleeting, I still, upon waking, understood that never before had I communed so painfully and so directly with God and my Christian faith.

A sense of solitude has been with me all my life, but I have fled from it, seeking refuge in ties with other people, so as to live with more dash and confidence. That morning I realized how very illusory those efforts had been. Seeing myself isolated in the world and in the presence of God, I realized how very defenseless I am. Then I was seized by a terrible fear. What meaning does my life have, I thought, in the face of the enormity of the world that has been given me in which to dwell? I am like a stray dog or a crippled horse abandoned in a trackless waste, or just a leaf fallen from a branch. I walk ahead thinking I know the direction, but that is a foolish delusion, for in fact I have no notion which way is east, west, north, or south. I plod along, not even leaving a footprint on this cruel and hostile earth, and I may well be constantly returning to the same place, unmarked and in no way distinct. Only my mounting fatigue allows me to take strength in the thought that I must be heading somewhere, that I have left something behind and that something else awaits me along the way. But when I look around or glance ahead, behind, or to the side, I always see the same thing: boundless and indescribable desolation, so spectral that the hair stands on my head and my heart shakes like a trapped bird. Here, there exists no measure for my endeavors, only time and space, only God filling everything with Himself, and I in His stony presence.

I remember that fearful morning: As I rose from bed, I made some noise, and my footman appeared in the doorway of my room. He was a person without charm whom I'd kept on a couple of years, more out of laziness than desire. Because of his inborn coarseness and stupidity, I had never found him amiable. But I am softhearted and delayed in dismissing him. Discharging a servant can be quite a disagreeable thing, so he remained in my home, always skulking a bit and looking intimidated. But he performed all his duties properly, in fear of the whip. I knew he did not like me in the least. But when he stood in the doorway that morning, glowering as he awaited instructions, I suddenly felt an inexpressible joy that he was there with me. And fear left me at once.

I do not know whether other members of the council had bad dreams, but they came to the town hall the next day at noon uneasy and excited, that I do know. That day, the Count de Saxe, Monsieur Meugne, and Monsieur de Vielle seated themselves farther to the side than ever before. At the time I thought this understandable and somewhat envied them. But can a windblown bush on a sand dune be compared with an oak or a beech tree? The de Saxe family arose from the soil of Artois ages ago. The de Vielles are descended from the crusaders whom Robert of Flanders led to the Holy Land. Monsieur Meugne, a man of extreme age, had looked after our Prince Philip when he was a child. Apparently, Monsieur Meugne had rendered Jean the Fearless inestimable services in his clash with the Armagnacs. And what was the Reverend Father Albert but an Italian stray compared to such people? He had bridled Arras with his ardent faith and exemplary ways, but that meant nothing to the proud lords who relinquished power to him, while maintaining their independence and a sense of superiority. When I was a student of the Reverend Father, I blossomed in his light. Some said I was Albert's better part, even his conscience. Even were it so, can a conscience exist without a person, and a part without a whole? And with these thoughts in mind, I took my usual seat to the left of the Reverend Father, though the others had seated themselves at a distance.

The session did not last long that day. The prologue is always short in form but long in content. It foreshadows what is to come. And so it was that day as well.

The Reverend Father raised his eyebrows and said, "It ill suits me to reproach men so nobly born as the Count de Saxe, and Messieurs de Vielle and Meugne. And that I will not do. But I cannot resist expressing surprise that on a day of such solemn importance as today, the most honorable men of our body have seated themselves at a distance, as if they felt themselves affronted and offended. This must be very grievous for the simple folk and cannot be called a truly Christian act."

De Saxe replied, "Good Father Albert, Monsieur Meugne is completely excused because of his age. He cannot sit in a drafty place. As for Monsieur de Vielle, he suffers from furuncles, and must get up and walk around several times during the session. And so as not to bother others, he has seated himself to one side." Then he fell silent.

Albert said, "All well and good. But what considerations moved you, my dear de Saxe?"

"That requires no explanation," said de Saxe. "I always sit wherever I wish. I'm unbelievably capricious by nature. And I always yield to my whims. And so any more talk on the subject, and my capricious nature will prod my butt until I stand and leave without so much as a bow to the distinguished council."

Albert seemed very angry but said no more on the subject. But the commoners reacted in a very singular manner to de Saxe's disquisition. They glanced at him with timorous respect, and at that moment, they would have granted his least demand. Yet he desired only to remain loftily apart.

Thus, the session began, but it did not last long. And before it was afternoon, old cases had been settled and new ones opened. Albert spoke of Tselus: "We should not insist that Tselus cast a curse on the house of the Damascene. However, the council should be aware that years ago, during the great plague, it was none other than Tselus who left town under very strange circumstances. He quit Arras almost immediately after the first victims succumbed to plague. Some people said that while leaving through Saint Aegidus' Gate, he kept repeating strange words, and that when he passed the bridge, he turned three times toward the town and made some secret signs. Mysterious are the dispensations of the Lord. We suffered a great deal here, yet none of us blasphemed Heaven because of our ordeal, because everyone understood that Arras's sufferings had been inflicted by Satan. God is mighty, but Satan is mighty too. We attempt to purify the town of everything that could favor the presence of the infernal powers, but it would be blasphemy to think that Arras belongs exclusively to God. Arras is a battlefield, a territory for whose conquest Heaven and Hell are locked in combat. God has His allies here, that is certain. But does not the devil have his as well? And who in Arras could be Satan's ally and hireling, if not those who do not commune with the

Lord God, do not obey the teaching of His Holy Church, and turn their backs contemptuously on the sacraments? Where is the devil gladder to cast his nets than among those who descend from the Pharisees? Whereas in other cities of Brabant and throughout the duchy, the Jews are deprived of privileges, here they enjoy a freedom that is sometimes greater than our own. We bow our heads before God's precepts, while they do not bend their necks even before the holiest of relics. Despite all that, during the plague Count de Saxe allotted the same amount of food for everyone, regardless of his birth. The Jews were refused neither food, nor care, nor worthy burial. And look what's come of it! In Ghent and Utrecht, where sin is a hundred times more common than in Arras, there was no suffering. We, on the other hand, could not have suffered more deeply. And what's the cause? Oughtn't one to think that God is displeased because we allow Satan to dwell within our walls and treat him with forbearance!

"So many of us died from plague and hunger that graves could not be dug fast enough. And what about the Jews? Well, I won't deny that they too lost some from the living. But how could it be otherwise. It was said that the Jews owed this to their superstitions. They huddled in their houses at the edge of town, by the Western Gate, kept apart from us by a guard. When they were given food, they performed some strange gestures before they would consume it. How can we be certain that all this was not the dictates of the devil? How can we be certain that they were not emissaries of the plague, whom Satan intended to save in order to make of Arras his court and capital? Imagine that the whole town had died and only the Jews were spared, that handful of Hell's allies. The churches soiled, the crosses trampled upon, the gates of Arras thrown wide to all iniquity. . . ."

Speaking very loudly, de Saxe interrupted this flood of rhetoric: "Reverend Father, those people should not be burdened with the guilt for the outbreak of the plague. There have been cases of plague befalling a town where a Jew had never once appeared. Nothing indicates they're responsible for what we suffered."

Albert nodded his head. "I'm not saying they're guilty," he replied mildly. "I'm only saying that anyone can be the instrument of God, and anyone can be the instrument of Satan. And is it not easier for the devil to ensnare a Jewish soul than a Christian one, and use it as a weapon of destruction against true Christians? Well, answer that, Count de Saxe."

De Saxe scowled, was silent for a long moment then finally said, "It is true that the Jew, devoid of the teachings of God's Church, is more easily subject to the promptings of Hell. Even so, God the Father also created the Jew, and for that reason, he deserves a bit of our trust."

The baker Mehoune cried out, "People say that during the plague three-headed dogs, spawned of

Hell, appeared by the Western Gate. They carried away any Christians who passed by there and brought them to the Jews to feast on."

"Three-headed dogs are servants of the devil. That is well known," interjected the clothier Yvonnet.

Then someone else added excitedly, "It cannot be that God punished the good town of Arras so severely for no reason. It didn't happen because of Heaven's will, but because of the devil's tricks. Has anyone in all the world ever seen pious people commit such infamies and iniquities as those we committed in the year of plague and hunger? Good citizens disemboweled others to have fresh meat on which to feed. Would our hearts have been capable of that if our town had not been ensnared by the devil? The unfortunate woman who murdered her child and who was executed by order of our good Albert had been driven to a madness that cannot be understood apart from the powers of darkness. Look at yourselves today. Does any of us nourish feelings of envy, anger, or contempt for others? We are good people, Jesus Christ lives in our hearts. But back then? Each of us sharpened his knife to cut his neighbor's throat. What can this be ascribed to, if not the devil's tricks that had taken possession of the town as a result of the Jew's curse."

"What are you driving at?" asked Albert.

He replied: "Sir, I am afraid that once again our leniency will result in terrible events. Again we have indulged the devil's fancies. You say that it was not proved that the Jew Tselus cast a curse on the home of the clothier that caused a horse of good blood to die. But three years before, there was also no evidence of what caused our cattle to die. Back then people said it was ill fortune or God's punishment. But punishment for what? Had the town of Arras sinned? Wasn't it full of prayer and the fear of God? At the time no one even thought that the cattle might have taken ill because of a Jew's curse. It was seen as the work of the Creator, a sign of fate, a decree from Heaven that could not be opposed. We offered up prayers, and we accepted the severest of trials with complete humility. Should we act in the same way today? Should the town be sent to its doom only because we cannot prove that Tselus was engaged in diabolical practices?"

And once again Albert said, "What are you driving at, my friend? Speak openly!"

He spoke: "Sir, our town should not be made the devil's prey. The Jewish community must answer for all its evil deeds!"

"They must answer for them!" shouted all the others, the baker Mehoune loudest among them.

Then Albert said, "But what if this is not the Jews' doing, and we do grievous wrong to the innocent?"

"Then God will absolve us because we acted with the intent of saving our souls," replied the clothier Yvonnet with great gravity.

Albert looked around and halted his gaze on my face. "Jan, my dear friend, what is your view?"

"Good Father," I replied, "Yvonnet puts the

question fairly. What can be more important for a Christian than to struggle for his salvation? If we err, God will count that to our good because our intentions are honorable. And that we are not free of hesitation attests to our humility."

After hearing me out, de Saxe, de Vielle, and Meugne rose and left the chamber. "Let them leave," said Albert. "They are such great lords that they can see to their own salvation without the council's help."

On the morning of the next day, the town of Arras began settling its accounts with the Jewish community. It was a rather misty and dreary day, not surprising at this time of year, but the mist caused people to remember the time of plague. As I have said, the town had been constantly shrouded in mist that year, and though the days had been quite warm, the nights had been cold enough for the water in shallow wells to congeal. But the plague had broken out in spring, while it was now autumn, and what might have seemed unusual in that season was only ordinary now. But human nature is at bottom extremely simple. It is in constant, anxious pursuit of signs that lend support to conscience. What is our life in the end if not the desire to justify our every act? Thus, since the town had realized that the Jewish conspiracy must finally be put to an end, thereby protecting Arras from Satan, everyone sought support, aid, and principles in the world around them. They did not at all head for the churches, as if prescient that their faith would offer them no justifications. Their faith lived on in their hearts, but it had

grown suddenly still, muffled by the need for justice
and action. A pale, cold sun that seemed covered by
cloth hung over Arras. Scraps of cloud passed low
over the town walls, as if a flock of great hostile night
birds were flying toward us. The church bells were
ordered rung, and the whole town resounded with
their ringing; but that day even the bells sounded
strange. For example, the bell in Saint Fiacre's
Church, which always rang with a pure and dignified
toll, now sounded very dull and muffled, as if it were
encountering some resistance. Later the bell ringers
were to tell that at the first tolling of the clapper, a
flock of black jackdaws flew out of the bell, followed
by the falling bodies of birds killed by the jackdaws,
a clear sign that the dark forces wished to silence the
bell at Saint Fiacre's Church.

Before the morning was over, the Jew named
Itzak was burning like a torch. Calm and determined,
people of various estates had come for him. There
was no need for shouts and threats. I was told later
that the Jewish community had humbly surrendered
its emissary. And he moved with the crowd toward
the place of execution, offering no resistance. Wood
and kindling were heaped around a stake, to which
Itzak was tied in a suitable fashion, so as not to cause
him needless suffering. The rope went around his
neck, but loosely, then around his chest and shoulders, and finally his shins. When the wood burst into
flame, people were silent, which is unusual. Everyone
was seized by the thought that they were about to
witness an extraordinary moment when the devil, de-

prived of his corporeal shell, must return to Hell. A terrible voice could be heard from within the flames. Some people said that they recognized the voice of the devil, but others doubted it. As for me, I think it was the suffering Jew crying out in his last hour. His body was examined when the fire went out, and indeed it was strange: The Jew seemed nearly untouched by the fire. Only his boots were burned to a crisp; his clothing, which had formerly been black, had turned the color of rust and mostly vanished, while his beard and the hair on his head had disappeared without leaving any ash. But there were no signs of the flames on his body, only strange red spots, as if something within him had been struggling to get out. His skin was cracked open in places, and so it was said that the devil had tried to butt through the Jew's chest with his horns but hadn't strength enough, and so remained within him and took the Jew with him back to Hell.

In the name of the Father, and of the Son, and of the Holy Ghost. Amen. I don't believe those stories, though I do admit I was prepared to grant them credence that day. But later on, there were so many purely human occurrences in which neither God nor Satan took part, that today I think that Itzak had nothing to do with Hell. If I am mistaken, God will absolve me of the sin.

What a terrible night followed that day. The sunset was violent; the entire horizon seemed soaked in blood. A warm, gusty wind drove in black clouds. The mob still filled the streets at twilight. Flares of torchlight lit up people's faces, white smears in motion, summoned from the darkness. It seemed to be a night of decision. The bells tolled ceaselessly, warning of danger, as in time of war or plague. A procession came singing from Saint Aegidus' Church, preceded by groups of flagellants emitting piercing cries. The men and women were naked to the waist, and their backs streamed with blood. Those walking behind struck those in front of them. Plaited thongs whistled in the air. Whoever fell was beaten until that person rose and continued in the procession. The penitents moved over ground wet with blood, over matted red straw, mud, and stone. The Jew Itzak was still tied to the stake at the place of execution.

I was on the steps of the church and looked with horror at this spectacle. Then I overheard a conversation between two people who had stopped near me in the shade of the church porch.

One said "Matthew, my good neighbor, I don't like what we're doing. I don't know if you can kill in the name of God. . . ."

"Shut your mouth!" replied Matthew sharply. "Anyone with doubts like yours is no good neighbor of mine."

Then the first said, "Why is that, Matthew? Jesus suffered on the cross for all of us. And when he was dying, he said in his agony, 'Father, forgive them, for they know not what they do!' If God spoke those words, is it fitting for one man to utterly condemn another?"

Matthew replied contemptuously, "God does

what He likes, but man is something else. Besides, apart from Heaven, what is of more value to us than our town?"

The one who doubted was silent for a long moment, then said, "I can see that you're right, Matthew. Don't blame me for what I said. I'm very glad that you rebuked me. I won't say it again."

Matthew replied in a boastful voice: "But you'll still think it?"

"Not at all, Matthew. I won't even think it. What I feel like doing now is spitting on a Jew's food." And the two of them walked briskly away.

I can't explain how it was that I followed them. They pushed their way through the crowd in the marketplace, then went toward the Western Gate where the Jews live. They were not alone. Though dusk had fallen, a great many people had gathered there, standing in silence around the Jews' houses. Their doors were all tightly shut, and there wasn't a sound anywhere, as if the people inside feared attracting misfortune.

Then the man whom Matthew had rebuked cried loudly, "Where is the elder of the Jews? Let him come out and face the citizens of the good town of Arras!" His cry was met with silence. And so he shouted again, this time seconded by a few others. That felt better than the stillness that had been before. Something began to happen: people seemed literally to come to their senses, becoming aware of their legs, arms, heads, necks. A few moved into a side street, lighting their way with torches. The torches sizzled with hostility, sparks bursting from them and falling into puddles where they were extinguished. Then a tangled mass of dried peapods caught fire, the flame bursting into the air and illuminating the whole street.

"It's the devil, the devil!" cried a voice from the crowd. People immediately cowered in fear; then, like a sea wave shattering an earthen embankment, they surged forward.

"The elder of the Jews!" they cried. "Where is the elder of the Jews?"

The houses of the Jews remained silent in fear. Not a murmur came from within them. Then suddenly, as an instant of silence fell on the billowing mob, our ears caught the sound of hoofbeats. By the light of the flames shooting high in the air, we caught sight of a rider in a dark cloak, his bay horse dashing from a side street and racing toward the Western Gate. A few citizens headed him off. They seized the horse by the bit and clung to its neck. Others pulled the rider to the ground. They dragged him along the straw-strewn street, pummeling him with their fists.

"He wanted to flee the town!" they cried. "Here's the deserter who wanted the good town of Arras to be the devil's prey."

The Jew said not a word. By the time they had dragged him to the marketplace, he no longer showed any sign of life. Still his body was tied to the stake, shoulder to shoulder with Itzak, and once again wood was brought and set afire.

While the flame was shooting upward, people shouted, "Here is the ally of Satan who wanted to open the gates of Arras to every iniquity."

The citizens then forced their way into the Jewish houses on the side streets near the Western Gate. An indescribable lamentation rose to the night sky, where a few scattered stars flickered sleepily. I walked to Saint Aegidus' Church. There was no one inside, and it was dark. I knelt down on the stone floor and prayed ardently.

In the name of the Father, and of the Son, and of the Holy Ghost. Amen.

Gentlemen, pay heed to what I am about to tell you. Here, in Bruges, I am like someone from another world. Your city has the reputation as a model of all the virtues, even though—as you yourselves say— there is less love and fear of God here than there are goods for sale. You belong to that special class of people who spend their days and nights in dark counting houses, or among creaking ships in a rich port. You deal with a vast world, one the people in Burgundy have no idea of at all. Your tables are heaped with unusual spices, flowers, and fruits that would no doubt evoke fear in the hearts of the citizens of my far-flung duchy. You set forth on distant voyages and have seen the peoples of this earth, with their yellow, brown, black, and light blue skins. You have so had your fill of wonders and horrors that there is no room in your hearts for any belief in the devil. We belong to another world. . . . When I arrived here and rode through the gates of the city, so hospitably open to me, I went at once to see the relics of Saint Ursula. And—can you imagine—I was the only person who had prayed before that holy altar in many years. Bruges is a much respected city, and I bow my head to your wisdom, enterprise, and wealth, but, believe me, we will never fully understand one another! I grew up on Brabant's succulent meadows and the teachings of the Holy Church, while you were sailing on distant seas. While I was fasting and doing penance, you were writing accounts of your adventures on enchanted islands, in the clime of gales, or at the ends of the caliph's lands. While I stood in faithful attendance on princes, you had the strength and courage to give offense to princes. I am grateful to you for harboring me and am filled with humility at being able to live in this most splendid city under the sun. But still I possess a treasure not given you. I have heard the voice of God and the voice of Satan. I have communed with Heaven and Hell. I know from experience what it means to battle for the salvation of one's soul. I have been through so much suffering, so many peaks and valleys, that you cannot fathom what my heart contains.

Gentlemen! I do not wish to deprive you of your illusions, but the truth is that a free person is not the one who is free, but the one who wishes to be so. Bruges is a great and rich city; but God has spared it a fall, and thus it cannot attain the sublime. You have placed your trust in your maps, ships, and captains. That is a good form of trust, but it does not of itself lead to salvation. I have heard that bodies have been dismembered in Bruges to discover what lies within a human being. In Arras we have done the same, but to a different end. We were moved by hunger, not curiosity. And it is for that reason that we know a hundred times more about man!

Hear me well. This will serve you in good stead, if not today, then tomorrow; and if not tomorrow, then the day after. . . . That night, while Arras resounded with the tumult of great slaughter, I was conversing with God and the devil. In the dim light of torches and oil lamps, alone and damned, I spoke with them both.

For years the Reverend Father Albert had been saying over and again that I owed the town of Arras a debt of gratitude, for it had raised me to the heights of success. Were it not for Arras, I might have been one of David's petty courtiers, or a balding abbot in some lucrative post. Arras had made me a co-ruler of all the people, animals, vegetation, goods, and property located within its walls. And so little was required in return: that I remain faithful to its laws and protect its privileges. By God, a paltry price for such a beautiful life.

Good sirs! Now prick up your ears. What does your city mean to you? Is it something you dream about at night? When one of you dreams of Bruges, you hear the creaking ropes of ships, smell seaweed and fish. Nimble gulls fly over roofs, hustle and bustle everywhere, endless pursuit. Bruges is like a bird, while Arras is like a tree. There, each person feels the roots of that tree in his very depths, just as here each person feels the lightness and freedom of a bird of passage.

That night in Saint Aegidus' Church, I was tormented by a question: what is my town really like? I wanted to see Arras in all the grandeur of its sin and virtue. Echoes of the slaughter reached me in the church, and I shuddered with fear and humility. This is my town, I told myself, but, believe me, it was God who said this.

The devil soon spoke up. "There is no other town like the town whose name is Truth," he said.

"And what is truth?" I asked in fear.

Then I heard the voice of God again. "I commanded Abraham to go out of Ur and abandon his own town, so not to have any desire but the desire for God. I tore Abraham's roots from his own soil, so that he would have no other soil but the soil of God."

What does that mean? I thought, beating my forehead against the cool stone floor.

Then I heard the devil whisper, "Jan! Settle in a town whose name is Jan."

The torches were slowly dying out, and the whole church was filled with the harsh smell of pitch. Now I was in darkness, only the weak oil lamp casting a flickering light from the altar. I was afraid that I was about to die and plunge into that darkness without having found any answer to my terrible questions. What would happen then? Where would my soul fly to? Does the road that leads to Heaven begin outside the walls of Arras, or right here amidst the shouts of my fellow citizens, in the glow of the fading stake, amid uproar and the neighing of frightened horses, in a feverishly whispered prayer and the groans of the flagellants at the church gates?

Oh, I knew that the citizens of Arras were doing evil and yielding to savagery. But after all I too had participated in their despair and their purification. Was I free to set my truths above the will of the town? I thought that this endless night was causing me terrible pain, and it was this thought that brought me relief: that I suffered from the faults of Arras meant that I had maintained my attachment to it.

Do not judge me too harshly. I am one of those who is wise enough to reject gratitude. I did not love Arras for feeding and clothing me, and placing some power in my hands, but because it suffered so. If you live with a town by day, you must dream with it by night. It was not Arras that was at fault, but God! "Jesus Christ, spare this town!" I cried, tears streaming from my eyes. "Do not inflict on Arras the fearful task of meting out justice, for there is nothing as terrible as passing judgment. Allow the town to weave tapestries as it did in the past, to tend its flocks, to trust in salvation. If the people of this town enter the street in which the stake burns, the fire will consume them all, because the search for justification is a passion stronger than the desire for a woman. O Christ, safeguard the town of Arras! Can you wish to make the town a victim of your repugnance for mankind. And, if You do, are there not other peoples, towns, and lands a hundred times more wicked?"

Then it seemed to me that God spoke very softly

and gently, as if to a capricious and foolish child: "Where is the certainty that Sodom was wicked? After all, Lot, a just man, lived there."

No, I said to myself, that could be the devil speaking in my heart. I will not be the Lot of this Sodom. I am strong enough to move Arras, but not strong enough to move God.

Just then, people entered the church, the clothier Yvonnet among them. "Jan's here!" he cried upon seeing me kneeling. "What's this? The town is shaken to its foundation, and you take shelter in a church? Good Father Albert is trying the elder of the Jews. You must go and throw your stone as well."

And so I went with them to the town hall. Neither Count de Saxe, nor Monsieur de Vielle, nor Monsieur Meugne was there. But the others were in the council hall, conducting the trial of the elder. When it came time for me to say what I thought, I replied loud and clear that the elder was guilty. And I did not sin in the least. The virtue of honesty cannot be turned against salvation.

But let us return to the point. I'm not supposed to be speaking of myself here, but of the town of Arras and its citizens.

Dawn was already breaking when sentence was passed. I went out to the marketplace, where I ran into de Saxe's steward, who was waiting for me. He said softly, "The Count de Saxe would like you to speak with him."

"What's happened?" I asked.

"That I don't know."

So we set off. People were wandering the streets. After the terrible exertions of the night, a few people had fallen asleep under the eaves of a building, in hallways, or on the church steps. A burning smell blew in from the Western Gate, where a few buildings had been reduced to ashes. As I walked, I came across two bodies, stripped of their clothing and badly maimed. The steward closed his eyes, and I caught an expression of fear and disgust on his fleshy face. He disappeared as soon as we arrived. Farias de Saxe was waiting for me in his garden, which was surrounded by a high wall. Tranquillity reigned there, and the air, raw that day, seemed mild and aromatic in his garden.

"Go to Bishop David," said Farias as we walked along a path between luxuriant bushes. "The bishop must know about everything that is happening."

"The town does not wish the bishop to come," I replied.

He glowered at me in great distress. "Jan, make haste for Ghent. One way or the other, all this business is connected to witchcraft. The town cannot pass sentences without its spiritual guide."

I spoke softly: "De Saxe, my friend, here in Arras we have our own rights and privileges, which should not be surrendered to the bishop's greed."

"You'd be right if this were a question of orchards, cattle, or grain, Jan, but it's human souls that are at issue here. No one granted the town the privilege of judging witchcraft and heresy." I said nothing, and he continued speaking. "I'm appealing to you because what better emissary to send to David's court? The bishop will listen only to you. And I also know that you will tell him openly what you think of all this wickedness. I'm not a young man, and so I understand the serious struggle that's being waged in your heart. You are very grateful to Arras, but just think: God is our Father, and the Church is our holy mother. . . . A mother should be especially gentle with her own children; however, she seems even crueler than the Father himself. Can this be allowed? I have received reports that many people were killed last night, and that Jewish homes were set on fire. They are alien to us, that is true. And that there is more evil in them than in Christian hearts is also true. Still, do not side with those who advocate violence. That's what I'm trying to tell you!"

Then I said, "Farias, what's happening in Arras clearly is meant to be. It is God who guides our acts."

"No," cried de Saxe with anger and despair. "God gave us reason, will, and fear. Ask God, Jan, and He will tell you that you can stay in Arras and join the violence, or you can go see David. The choice is yours."

"My hope is in God," I replied softly.

Farias de Saxe pulled out a short knife and cut a sprig of alder. Its sticky sap ran into his hand and trickled to the ground. Then, as if speaking to himself, he said, "You're not the first, Jan, nor are you the last. Such is life here on earth. I've heard tell of a woman by the name of Margôt, who lived in olden times, and who thought that her soul was entirely absorbed in

God. She could no longer sin, because God Himself guided her actions. They say she was a very honorable woman, even though she was burned in Paris for her wicked heresy. There are other cases. Some people said that they were so annihilated by God that their every gesture, step, and word issued from the will of God. If they drank, God drank through their lips. If they raped, God guided their wanton erection. If they killed, God raised their sword. So, tell me, could there be any annihilation sweeter than that? A person indulges his every desire, but always remains pure as a child, for he is only the instrument of God. You say that it is the will of Heaven that iniquity take place in Arras. Then let God grieve over the blood spilled and forgive Himself His own sin. . . . How I envy you! As for me, I am tormented by every cry that reaches me from the street. Do you really think that anything happens in isolation from you?"

"I'm in God's hands!" I replied in a severe tone.

He glanced at me, then went on cutting alder branches. "But He is also in your hands, Jan, because you desire His grace so greatly. He desires your salvation."

"You're talking like a heretic!" I cried in horror.

He looked at me again, a bit wary, a bit plaintive, and said, "You see God as having the mouth of a wolf and fangs sharp as knives. He devours you in His insatiable hunger, and you are only meat for His famished jaws. And all Arras does the same. It yields to iniquity, but remains without sin, believing it's only doing God's will. We have no meaning, people say to each other on the street, since we are only miserable worms, playthings of God's will. And in that way you place all your sins on God's shoulders. That's so easy, Jan! Soon there will be nothing left of you because you will have relinquished everything to Heaven."

I walked away without saying a word. When I turned, he was looking at me from afar, alone in his garden.

It was a day without end. The elder of the Jews was executed in the afternoon. Again people began moving toward the Western Gate. Something insatiable was consuming our hearts. The desire to serve the town had been roused in every citizen. Once again a few Jewish homes went up in flames. Cries, prayers, and curses mingled, and, above it all, the sound of bells shook the air.

The council met late in the day. Albert greeted us with a nod. I had not seen him the whole day, and now he seemed strangely weary and dejected, as if entire years had passed since early morning. The only light I saw in him was in his eyes. He spoke: "The council should pay close attention, for I have decided to confide in you. First, because today is a special day for Arras, one never to be repeated. I am an aged man. I came to Artois from far away in the south, not so much to satisfy my own heart as to obey orders from the authorities. When I first entered the gates of Arras, I was very young, and you who hear me now were little children. And so, I have spent my life teaching you the Christian virtues. I wanted only one thing—that the town be pleasing to God. Soon it will be time for me to die and leave this world. And so this morning I gave thought to what I had accomplished, and what I had failed to accomplish. Is Arras better now than it was on the day I arrived here? What have you gained from my teachings and my humble example? Well, it probably can be said that I instilled in you faith in God and His saints. Under my guidance, you have cleared your own narrow path to Heaven. That path is tortuous, stony, steep. And the climb is not an easy one. Sometimes a person will stand on the side of that path, and look down and up. He is horrified that he has gone so little of the way, and feels like turning back, for it is easier to live in the lowlands than on the heights. Down there you can indulge your every whim, whereas when climbing, you must think of only one thing—how not to fall and be smashed to bits. I tell you, the whole world has conspired against our town, for it envies us our communion with God and all the other experience we have been vouchsafed. And that is the reason why people sometimes grumble when their wagons that bore serge to Lille or Calais return empty to the gates of Arras. Those people think the great world full of amusement and temptations that are easy to satisfy. In Arras, however, the stubborn struggle for salvation awaits them once again. So, some say, 'Why do we need the teachings of good Father Albert if we only have one life? Others indulge themselves all they can and, in the hour of their death, repent their sins and close their eyes in the hope that God will forgive them.' This is what some citizens say. They don't realize that the devil is

speaking through their lips. Yesterday we put the
Jews on trial. And what do I see? The citizens of Arras
came to the conclusion that the Jews would pay all
the debts Arras had contracted in Heaven. . . . By God,
it's impossible to think of anything as foolish and
comical as that. What is the source of the evil that
festers in our town? The baker Mehoune argued that
the Jews were the source, which I do not deny. But tell
me, Mehoune, my dear brother, in tearing out the
Jewish evil, do we also tear out its roots that took
hold in Christian souls? Should we hide from the face
of God behind the Jew? Is that not an attempt at
deception, or playing dice with Jesus Christ? Certain
citizens suppose that they can hide behind Jewish
corpses and not be seen by the eye of Providence.
The poor fools! In setting Jewish houses on fire, they
delude themselves that, as in Purgatory, the fire will
whiten their souls. They are moved by fear and wish
to avoid true judgment at any cost. Those who are not
themselves innocent are the fiercest in persecuting
the people who live by the Western Gate. Oh, how
they desired to drown their own iniquities in Jewish
blood. God does not absolve sins that were vented,
but those that were redressed. He is not satisfied with
words but demands deeds. We have surrounded
Arras with a wall of Jewish bodies, and we think we
are safe. Meanwhile, we are in a peril, the likes of
which the world has never imagined. Gervais the
Damascene came to us and said that the Jew Tselus
cast a curse on his house and farm. Maybe that was
so, and maybe it wasn't. Where is it written that God

cannot punish a man by taking away his horse? I do not maintain in the least that Tselus was innocent. I maintain only that the horse could just as well have died without his curse. God has no need whatsoever of Jewish help when He wishes to mete out justice. Arras was not a good town before the plague afflicted us. Terrible things were happening here. It has been said at the council that more grievous and baser sins occur in Ghent, Breda, and perhaps even in Paris, but it was on us that plague was inflicted. But does the council have the right to judge the sins of others? And what if it pleases God to annihilate Brabant and all the duchy's other lands in order to spare a single village, as once happened with Noah and his ark? Let us reckon our own sins and seek our own measure! Just cast your mind back—was there so little perfidy, lust, and foolishness in Arras? Was it not said in the town that the baker Mehoune added sawdust to his flour, and that Yvonnet the clothier cheated the Widow Placquet, who works as a servant in his house? And did not the best among us—even Count de Saxe —keep English women of easy virtue and abandon themselves to dissipation? Even my favorite student indulged abominable passions before the very eyes of the entire town! Let the council weigh my words: I am telling you that it is easy to repent your sins with the blood of Jews, but that need not at all be pleasing to God."

The chamber grew hushed when Albert ceased speaking. Evening had already fallen, and through the windows all that could be seen were the burning houses by the Western Gate. The baker Mehoune rose from his bench, his body casting a large shadow on the wall. The baker spoke: "Good Father, I have sinned grievously, because the truth is I did add sawdust to the flour. I will pay for a hundred masses at the Church of the Holy Trinity and lash my back on every fast day."

"A good Christian does not impose his own penance," replied Albert. Mehoune fell to his knees and burst into loud tears.

"Don't cry, for your hour has not yet come." said the Reverend Father in a very gentle voice. "Stand up, Mehoune, and we will continue our deliberations." Mehoune rose and returned to his seat.

It is unbelievable how devoid of thought we were that night. I suppose every man bears his own burdens and does not feel them overmuch. But there comes a time when a piece of straw tossed onto his shoulders causes his whole body to bend to the ground; his breath becomes shallow, sweat streams into his eyes, and all his feelings turn to an animal desire for rest: only to throw off that burden, only to be free of that weight. At the time we don't recall that it is no more than a piece of straw pressing on us, for it feels as if the whole earth, and even the whole sky, has been loaded onto our shoulders. Then everyone looks around anxiously for a place to cast that burden; and when he catches sight of a neighbor, he burdens him with it, and in good conscience!

When Mehoune had resumed his seat, the others regarded him with sneers and hostility. Everyone had wanted to weep, but Mehoune was the first to do so, which allowed the others to regain some calm. He had been the first of them to display humility, but they were not grateful to him, or rather they were filled with both gratitude and hatred. A shudder went through me as I recalled what Albert had said about that English girl I'd been with many years ago when I was supposed to be working on a commentary on the writings of Master Gerson. I glanced at the faces of the people in the council chamber, but all their faces were twisted in humble prayer. Their whispers, crackling like a flame enveloping dry wood, resounded in the chamber. God had plenty of work to do at that moment—to hear so many sins confessed at once. Still, they were praying. I had never seen people in such rapture. It was as if an entire monastery of Carthusians had swarmed into the town hall, and yet I knew them! Knew them better than my own mares and stallions. Oh, they weren't bad people at all. No worse than any others in Burgundy. It was just that they had been so suddenly caught between Heaven and Hell; it was all so unexpected and with no time to prepare. Who among us has not committed some evil in his life? Usually people know when they sin, but it rarely occurs to them that they could be put to the test as described in Scripture. That sort of thing might have happened in olden times or might not have happened at all. But it is not of paramount importance whether God revealed Himself one way or another. Faith is a part of human nature, not of divine nature. God does not have to believe in Himself; it is

us who must have faith in Him! These were religious
people, which does not mean however that every day
they remained God's most faithful lambs. They
behaved as people usually do. They knew they would
have to pay for their every act but could never have
thought this would happen that very night, in the
council chambers, by the light of dying fires. The
Church teaches us that we do not know the day or the
hour, but precisely because we do not, we are able to
remain calm and retain a modicum of dignity. When
times like these suddenly befall us, we feel helpless
and deceived. And so it was that night. All I could hear
in the stillness of the town hall was the whisper of
prayerful lamentation. If the devil was among us at
that moment, he did not make a murmur. Who knows
in whose cloak he was lurking?

I leaned toward Albert and said, "Father, I must
leave the council hall!" He nodded. I rose and went to
drink some water from the well in the courtyard. It
was cold outside and very dark. I drank greedily, im-
mersing half my face in the bucket. Then something
touched my shoulder, and I turned slowly around.
There was no one there. I drank some more water, for
my innards were on fire, probably from fear of Albert,
the council, the whole town of Arras. Once again I felt
a light touch on my shoulder. I let go of the bucket,
which fell downward, still hanging from the resilient
hemp rope, until I heard water splash at the well's
bottom. I looked everywhere but saw nothing. Only
the faint outline of the town hall. Suddenly, a whisper.
Someone was speaking in my ear, but I couldn't un-

derstand the words, as if they were in a foreign language I had never encountered before. "Who's there?" I asked in fear. Again a voice uttered outlandish words that I would not even be able to repeat today. Words without a mouth, speech without a person, a touch without a hand, a part without a whole. Something that felt like a fist struck my chest. Covered in sweat, I took flight but could feel a boot kicking me in the seat of my pants. It was the devil driving me with kick after kick right to the doorway of the council chamber! I burst into the chamber, all eyes on me. My face must have been deathly white and my eyes completely glazed. "The devil is in the town hall!" I cried in a terrible voice and with the last of my strength slammed the council door shut. The others fell to their knees, the hair on their heads standing on end.

Even Albert seemed anxious. He drew near the door and made the sign of the cross over it. I could hear him mutter to himself, "The devil's in the town hall . . . the devil's in the town hall. Who knows?"

In the name of the Father, and of the Son, and of the Holy Ghost. Amen. Gentlemen! Even now my flesh creeps as I recall drinking that water in the courtyard. A spring sun is shining over Bruges today, and through the window I can see a ship with its sails unfurled on a broad expanse of water. Your faces are peaceful and honorable; for lunch we had an exquisite turkey pie and a leg of lamb. Still, I'm feeling thirsty again and would like some fresh water to rinse old fears from my throat. Gentlemen! If anyone asks if I've seen the devil, the answer is "no." But if anyone asks if I have heard his voice and felt his touch, the answer is "yes"—my backside is still sore from his kicks.

Oh, but that does not mean in the least that I claim that everything that happened last autumn in Arras was the work of the powers of darkness. But the devil was constantly afoot there, taunting us, fanning the dying flames of the stakes, clouding our minds, and nudging us toward our doom. We would have hit bottom even without him, but probably not so rapidly.

I'll return to my account. That same night the council demanded that Albert have Farias de Saxe arrested. For a long time he objected. "He is the highest born man in all Arras!" he repeated doggedly. But the council would not yield. Yvonnet the clothier argued that de Saxe had committed evil and abominations in the year of the plague. Clearly he was in league with the Jews since he had fed them so well when others had nothing to put in their mouths.

Albert replied, "Leave the Jews out of it! They have paid what they owed. If our own evil and misfortune had its source only in the Jews, the town of Arras would be a hundred times happier. Alas! Seek sin in your own hearts, and leave the Jews out of it!"

It was not difficult to prove that de Saxe was among the most hardened of sinners. Who else but de Saxe had been mocking the Reverend Father's teachings for years and years? It was discovered that he had brought a medical student to Arras from Worms, and, at night, by torchlight, they dissected the bodies of dead animals. Farias de Saxe caught lizards in the ravines between Arras and Lille, removed their skins, and examined their innards. He did the same with birds, and it is said, not without basis, that during the plague when he divided up the meat from a dead horse, he kept the heart for himself. He did not eat it but examined it, weighed it, dissected it, and marveled at it. Everyone knew that Farias de Saxe was bored to death in Arras and would have holy mass said in his own chambers at night because he was out hunting with his falcons in the daytime. He was very lax about making confession and would sometimes doze off while confessing, requiring the father to physically prod him into repenting his sins. And when he received communion, his whole body would shake and he would yawn protractedly. It was established beyond any doubt that de Saxe kept corrupt women in his house and each night selected a different one, like an Arabian caliph. But, most importantly, he did not respect the council, behaved in very lordly fashion at its sessions, and cared nothing for the Reverend Father's teachings. He had made this especially clear in recent times when commoners began to take part in council sessions; he slighted them and would not deliberate with them. Gentlemen, I think that the Count de Saxe was undoubtedly right, but should not have displayed his attitude so openly to the riffraff themselves.

In the end, Albert yielded. He nodded his head and said softly, "Since this is the will of the council, I humbly join in it. We will put the Count de Saxe on trial, and that may win us Heaven's grace. I will tell you once again, my dear fellow citizens, anyone of great experience can no longer be pure. Absolution is granted only to the inexperienced and the unknowing. The time of hunger and plague soiled our souls. The town of Arras probably had to burn in the flame of suffering in order to regain its true health. Every step took us farther and farther from the right path and sank us deeper in the mud. Today we need a child's faith in order to enter onto the path of virtue. Before plague befell the town, people gave more energy to the making of beautiful tapestries and serge, to horses and orchards, to ducats and barrels of wine, than to their own salvation. The plague opened our eyes to what is truly important to man. And when the plague passed, vice again took up residence within the walls of Arras. Once again people dealt in linen and flax, horses and cows, and drove wagons full of goods to Calais. The town was consumed by the desire for ornate utensils and fine food, swift horses and milch cows. The only things discussed were falcons, boots, and hats. And only a handful of the bravest dared to cry out that we also needed God. People had fallen so low in their desire to grow rich that even the worthiest of men committed infamies. There was one man in Arras who was even in collusion with bandits. On his orders, they would lie in wait in the hills along the road to Lille and rob our wagons of their goods. These were the same people who during the plague rode up to the walls of the city to plunder our food."

"Reverend Father!" cried Mehoune the baker. "Who was the man who hired the robbers?"

"That I will not say," replied Albert. The council then began loudly to curse this refusal to trust them. Once again people fell to their knees, and their voluble prayers resounded to the very ceiling. Finally, Albert said very softly, with what seemed much effort, that it had been the Count de Saxe.

"Hell!" screamed Yvonnet, and others seconded his cry.

"Yes," replied Albert. "Hell is in us all." At the time I thought, but kept it to myself, that indeed Hell resides in us, but the Hell we have created in the world around us is a hundred times worse.

Gentlemen, you are aware that the Count de Saxe was burned at the stake last autumn in Arras; but you are not aware how much he blasphemed before his death and what results that had for our town. When the count was imprisoned in the town hall's cellars, his steward, Durance by name, whom I have already mentioned, appeared before the council and announced that he wished to defend his master, saying, "He is not guilty of the accusations against him!" That Durance was always a strange person. Sometimes he acted like the lowest rogue. Before the plague broke out, Durance had made a long journey on business, going as far as the Rhône Valley. Upon his return, he told how he had fleeced the people there. He was perfidious to such an extent that even in Brussels Prince Philip heard complaints about his behavior.

He got away with it that time because he was under the protection of the Count de Saxe, who enjoyed the prince's favor. On another occasion, he gained fame throughout Artois by giving one hundred ducats to the Carthusian monastery. All in all, he was a generous man, even more than he appeared. It was said that he had paid for presents given to the English nuns in Bedford and transported them across the sea himself in a ship he had hired. He gave charity to widows and orphans, but would reduce a debtor to beggary. He was elegant of speech and physique. He was an enormously wealthy man: his fortune probably exceeded that of Farias de Saxe, whom he continued to serve. At times he would feed de Saxe's horses with his own hands, something he never did for his own horses because he had his own stableman and several grooms. Sometimes he lived like a model Christian, fasting and praying, but at other times he could give himself over to debauches that were the talk of the town. He kept a shaveling and two concubines. People say that once he took the shaveling for the night and in the morning confessed this to the women. No one knew what really lay within the man, and some people feared him a little.

When he came to the council, he had a stoney air about him and spoke with enormous haughtiness. He knew that since he was not himself being tried but defending Count de Saxe, he was, for the time being, free to act as he pleased, a privilege of which he made full use: "What is it you want from the noble de Saxe? From whose hands did you receive food for yourselves and your bastards in the time of hunger and plague? At that time you yourselves cried out there was no worthier and no more just man in all Arras. Albert, listen to me. If in fact fate is now putting us to the test over those poor Jews and Monsieur de Saxe —and something tells me that this idiocy will not end with the count—the fault should be sought in ourselves. Do you remember the cry of the woman to whom you refused to lend comfort on the scaffold? If you've forgotten, God will remind you. People! Who are you listening to? Look at that old man at the head of the table. You call him the 'Reverend Father,' but I tell you he's a stinking old goat who's sick of life and the whole human race. What does he want? While we're enjoying the sun and the rain, the flowers and the leaves, he's thinking of sulphur and the devil's pitchfork. Before the plague, the town suffered greatly because of him. We may sometimes have lacked grain, but we never lacked chasubles. Every last human sound has died out in this town; all that is heard is prayer. There is too much faith here and too little intelligence. Is that what God wants? We are His children, and why then would He wish our humiliation and misery? That old gray ram should leave the good town of Arras. He should hand over power to enlightened people who are able to unite piety and common sense. Otherwise, this old man will create such a hell for you that stone will not be left on stone in Arras!"

Albert listened but said not a word. When Durance had concluded, Albert said only, "Citizens, judge for yourselves what you must do!" The council ordered the steward to leave the chamber. It was already clear that he would be the next to stand trial.

The commoners on the council demanded that de Saxe repent his sins, but he refused. How could he have done otherwise? I went to see him that evening and said that if he avowed his sins and displayed contrition, the council was prepared to sentence him to banishment from the town. Otherwise, he would burn at the stake.

De Saxe laughed bitterly and said, "Listen, Jan, I know what the town wants today. It wants a battle! People imagine they'll find purification in the fire of battle. They inflict violence on others to free themselves from the nightmare oppressing Arras. They're entangled in the devil's meshes even if their intentions are good. If I tell them today that I sinned by conspiring with bandits and by blaspheming God, I'll be part of all this madness. Better to die than have a hand in that. I do not desire martyrdom in the least, but I do know that there is nothing worse under the sun than to confess to wrongs you have not committed. Anyone who loves God and man will not yield to such demonic temptations."

"If you do not display humility, you'll die tomorrow."

De Saxe regarded me intently and must have seen only the outline of my face, as it was so dark in the dungeon. He said, "I know, but I'm not a young man. Everyone's time comes. God will forgive because He can see into my heart. And it's pure, Jan."

"De Saxe, my friend," I spoke ardently. "You know how close I am to you. I think of Albert as a father, and you I have always thought of as a brother. Trust me. Your death will not change the town. You'll die in vain!"

"That may be," he replied softly. "But if I remain alive, a great deal will change. People will conclude that they had been right, and their image of sin will be drawn tight as a bowstring. But the human mind is not a bowstring and should not be drawn taut. When it breaks, Arras will descend into madness. It is a good town, Jan, and it deserved a better fate. I do not wish to be the executioner of this town. Better the town be mine."

He said the same thing again and again, which was not entirely wise. Leaving the cell, I thought the count was deceiving himself. How high a value did he place on his dignity? One so high that I could detect the sin of pride in it.

It was already night when I began walking home. The town was asleep, the fires had died out, everything was hushed. The wind murmured gently in the treetops, and the sky was clear overhead; probably the first time that autumn that it hadn't been overcast. I walked at a brisk pace. Here are my legs, I thought, here are my feet, knees, shins, loins. They move in cadence, for that is what I wish, though I do not bid them so. They know what to do. Life is so marvelously complex, the human body above all. Anyone who consigns his own body to the flames is a traitor. . . . Here is my stomach, I thought, here are my shoulders, my head, my eyes, mouth, hair. Every hair of mine feels the stirrings of the wind. When it rains, my hair gets wet and yields with delight to my fingers' caress. And my fingers take pleasure in the feel of that rough, damp hair. Each part of me lives its separate life, yet all together constitute a single person. This is the true miracle of creation. When I run, I feel how distinct is each part of my body. At first, there is a light stinging in the feet, but I feel vigorous and cheerful. Then, if I keep running, a mild shudder runs from my calves to my knees, which absorb it. Then my legs become as heavy and lazy as those of a pregnant woman, but my stomach, arms, and shoulders still feel like running. After a while, my breath becomes shallow, my mouth dry, and my head throbs with pain. Then my legs refuse to obey. In vain do I bid them to move faster, for they've had enough of me, and I'm a stranger to them now. They are as separate as if they'd been hacked off with an ax. But all it takes is a minute of rest, a sip of fresh water, for them to merge with the rest of my body and start moving again, obedient, confident, unfailing. My good legs, I thought, my beloved arms, hands, and innards. How could I ever dare deliver you to doom and destruction! I am your master and servant, friend and lover, benefactor and tyrant. Cleave to me, and together we shall survive all the vicissitudes of fate. Nothing is more important than survival.

As I walked home, I thought that in the morning the sun would rise and the whole sky turn a glorious rose color. Then that rosiness would vanish, and Arras would bask in the sun's golden rays. A quarrelsome, hostile wind might blow in, jostle the leaves, fan the flames of the stake where Farias de Saxe burns, blow off someone's hat, or steal away a wisp of straw. I shall drink milk at noon as I do every day. My manservant will bring me a mug of warm milk, straight from the cow's udder, which I will drink, sitting comfortably. Then I will go to the council and in the evening order my dinner—a leg of mutton, beer, cheese and fruit, then drink warm milk again, from the late milking. At day's end I will lay down my legs, arms, shoulders, stomach, and head in my bed and summon one of the women in my household to bring me easement.

Can there be anything as worthy as staying alive? Did God create us to annihilate ourselves in the name of various delusions? Freedom is much discussed nowadays. In the time of our ancestors it was knightly honor that was spoken of everywhere. In his youth, my great uncle saw the picture of a certain lady and swore himself to her service. For three decades he wandered through nearly every land on earth, lived the life of a shepherd, slept under the open sky, and ate only peas and radishes. Wherever he went, he would at once relate fantastical tales of his lady and fight in tournaments. He suffered many broken bones, which pained him greatly, but he remained true to his oath. Learning at last where to find his beloved, he boarded a ship and sailed to Benevento, in Italy. There, he was welcomed by a sinewy old dame who stank like a dung heap, and who was much impressed by his proofs of chivalry. My great uncle died in her arms, crying out before his death that he was very glad not to have wasted his life, having seen at its end the lady of his heart. When his armor was removed, he supposedly had thirty wounds on his body that he had suffered in jousts for his lady.

That tale moved me greatly when I was young, but, as I grew up, I grew wiser. While my great uncle was roaming the world, that strumpet from Benevento was able to marry three times and have a dozen sons. Very nice! But the worst of it is that no one forced that knight to pursue such a vile trollop.

But all that was long ago, and today we laugh derisively at such folly. But do we not harbor folly in our hearts? Freedom! I was always for freedom. I've already spoken of that. But, in today's world, when some people speak of respect for man, freedom of conscience, inquiry, and thought, I cry as loudly as possible for freedom for my loins, arms, knees, hair, tongue, stomach, nostrils, fingers, lips, ears, feet, elbows, liver, teeth, bones, and anus. Oh, I swear, gentlemen, all this is so terribly much mine, so painfully mine, like nothing else could ever be! The Creator Himself entrusted me with this body so that I would safeguard its right to exist.

· All I know is that the Count de Saxe betrayed his own body and thus the person given him by God. Gentlemen, may God rest his soul though he did sin grievously.

The worst of it came when he was taken out for execution: He cried to the people gathered in the streets that he was innocent and was dying to awaken the good town of Arras. "May God absolve you all as I absolve you!" he said, which every thinking person took as rank blasphemy. Such words were becoming to Jesus Christ, but not to the Count de Saxe, a hardened sinner. And so people picked up stones, clumps of dry mud, horse manure, and goat droppings and threw them at him. All the same, he kept his countenance and maintained an impressive dignity. As he was being tied to the stake, he said to the executioner loudly enough for all to hear, "Master, do your job well. I'm giving you a ducat for that." The executioner bowed deeply and kissed the count's boot though it was covered with manure. And he did his job well—I would even say too well. And he did so in order to enjoy his ducat all the sooner. Having tied the count to the stake, he set the wood on fire; when it burst into flame, the executioner very adroitly plunged his knife into the count's heart. De Saxe groaned and at once gave up the ghost. Thus, the fire consumed an already unfeeling body. However, this was seen by the people standing near the stake, who reported it to the council; and so Arras's town executioner was the next to be executed, although it was some time later. Truly, he died a happy man because with that ducat, his wife was able to purchase a pretty piece of property by Trinity Gate and was thus well provided.

In the name of the Father, and of the Son, and of the Holy Ghost. Amen. I experienced some very painful moments on the square that day. It took the greatest efforts to suppress the sobs struggling to escape my breast. A great and good man, a worthy friend and protector, had left this world. I had been the last to speak alone with him. After I had visited him in the dungeon, he was brought before the council, to which he refused to show repentance, instead calling on its members to come to their senses. And so I can consider myself the last person in whom Farias de Saxe confided before his death. I prayed ardently to God that He accept this errant soul into Heaven. But it was just while I was praying, in broad daylight on the square as the stake went up in flames, that doubt began to haunt me. I was so close to being reconciled to everything happening around me when suddenly a terrible thought occurred to me. I glimpsed the face of Christ on the Cross, pale and contorted by suffering. Then I could see the face of Pontius Pilate, who was washing his hands. And the face of Paul who had denied the Lord. I had had a vision of that sort once before. Chastell and I were hunting in the woods outside Ghent. That was in my youth when the English ruled nearly the entire coast. Chastell fell from his horse and was so badly injured that no one would have predicted he would survive. We came upon a peasant at the edge of the woods and lay Chastell on some haulms. He cried for water, and the peasant's boy ran to the well. I then said, "Chastell, my old friend, you need a confessor. I'll send the peasant for one of the Jacobin fathers."

"Don't do that," said Chastell, forcing a smile. "I

don't want to make confession. . . ." He must have seen by my eyes that I thought him mad, because he went on to say, "I never thought I would die in your company, far from my older, wiser friends. But there's no escaping fate. I don't want any cleric here. You know me, dear boy, and so you know I always scoffed at Christian practice and cared nothing for God's commandments. Not that I am an evil man. Not at all! But I don't believe in God. I never went to church, I never bowed low to the altar, never confessed my sins. I don't believe in any of that. . . ."

I froze with horror. To tell the truth, Chastell's atheism was public knowledge at the court of Ghent, and more than one great lord followed his example. Prince Philip himself said that Chastell was a most honorable and most noble man, and thus God lost much in such a man's refusal to believe in Him. But all that was on this shore, and now Chastell was floating swiftly toward that other shore where there is no longer any place for pranks and poses. Consequently, I saw no reason to delay; a confessor should be called at once. But he didn't let go of my hand.

"Pay close heed to what I'm telling you, boy!" he whispered with difficulty. "My heart has not been filled with atheism, but with the certainty that I will turn to dust, fall into a boundless darkness where it is vain to seek beings of any sort. And so even now, when my mind is shaken by the strange idea that maybe I will yet find something there, I wish to persevere in my faith. If there's no God, what do I need a Jacobin father for? And if there is a God, what would

He think of me? That I fell on my knees before Him, out of fear, at the last moment? If God exists, He is wise and great. And if He is wise and great, He scorns fools and the fainthearted. And that is why I will not go out and meet Him halfway!"

The boy returned with the water. I did not send the peasant to the monastery. Chastell spent the whole night in an airless room. He did not even moan. I sat by the door listening to his breathing. That night was very cold, and all my limbs shivered. A horrible fear seized my heart, and that was the first time I glimpsed that uncanny trinity, Our Lord Jesus Christ, Pilate, and Peter. The second time they appeared to me was last autumn when Farias de Saxe was dying. I swear I don't know what it could mean; but I do know that it spread immense unrest in me and, what's worse, deprived me of clarity of mind, as if I had become a vessel from which a precious liquid leaked. Sometimes I ask myself what is the source of a person's courage and prudence. One can accept the simplest answer, namely that God endows some people with daring in action and in thought, and not others. But which ones? Some people say it is the wellborn, but that I don't believe because in my time I have seen so many cowardly men among the lordly. Let us even take Durance, de Saxe's steward, and set him beside Chevalier du Losch.

I have not yet spoken of this, for it's not worth speaking of at all! Du Losch put on a real performance when he was brought before the council. As Mehoune listed du Losch's misdeeds aloud, du Losch roared,

"It's true, esteemed council, all true! I am the lowest sinner in the world." When the listing of his misdeeds was complete, he added a great many himself, heaping such filth upon himself that even the commoners looked away.

Finally Albert asked, "Is that all, du Losch?"

At first he agreed, but appearing to think intensely, as if forcing himself to remember, after a moment he cried, "Esteemed council, when I was a child, I had relations with a goat."

Then even Albert burst out laughing. I thought that du Losch was mocking us, but he was repenting out of a heartfelt need. He had miscalculated, the poor wretch! He had hoped to win himself a flogging by wagging his tail. But, after being grandly amused, the council ordered him beheaded. On hearing the sentence, he burst into tears and fell to the ground, where he groveled and clutched at the legs of the baker Mehoune, his accuser.

Then a terrible thing happened. The baker said, "Monsieur du Losch! Remember who you are! A chevalier should not cling to a baker's calves."

When du Losch was executed, no one in Arras so much as mentioned his name. Durance, though of low birth, did however have the courage to go to his death with his head held high. He cursed Albert, spat at his feet, and even while the flames were licking at his body, he cried out to the Reverend Father, "Come over here, you old goat, so I can fart in your face!"

In the end, what is the truth of valor and discretion? If God has no hand in it, then they must be human things. Chastell used to say to me, "Be the master of your own fate!" Oh, I know, that's all that counts, but now I can say that I have never been satisfied on that score. Sometimes I was the master of my fate, and sometimes I wasn't. At times I was tormented by the desire to cry out, regardless of what might happen, and yet I held my tongue. At other times, I was seized by some destructive force and ready to lay my head on the chopping block if only to save something that I could not even name. Gentlemen, isn't the point to please oneself, even more than to please God?

I can see by your faces that I'm beginning to bore you. That's understandable, considering that what I say differs so much from the usual conversation here in Bruges. I bare my heart, but to you it's noise and air. Then let us return to our rams, the rams of Brabant!

Two days had not passed since the death of de Saxe when all Arras resounded with savagery and murder. The town was swept by trials for witchcraft, heresy, and the most abominable perversion. Life lost all certainty. Some cases reached the council; others were handled outside its jurisdiction. Gervais the Damascene, whose horse was killed by Tselus's curse, was dragged from his house by his debtors and strung up. His stables were put to the torch.

At the council, Albert had said that only the simple folk would enter Heaven, words that were immediately turned against all the wellborn. But don't think this became a plebeian revolt! Nothing of the sort could happen in Arras. The people there are too lazy-minded for any of that. It was just that the people thought that those of higher station must be more entangled in the devil's snares than those of lower. There was no talk of equality in Arras during those days. It was rather that many people had a sudden hankering to drink from the lords' vessels and to dress in their clothes. The most respectable men, like the wheelwright Tomas the Lame, whom I'd known for a long time, turned to brigandage. With a gang of servants, Tomas broke into Monsieur de Vielle's chambers, tied him to a ceiling beam, and questioned him like a judge: "In what way did you blaspheme?"

"I didn't blaspheme," said Monsieur de Vielle.

"If I say you blasphemed, then you did."

"But I didn't!" insisted de Vielle.

"You won't get off easy this time," said Tomas. "The Reverend Father Albert has placed the simple folk of Arras in charge of meting out justice. We most fervently love God and will leave no sin unpunished."

"And what makes you one of those simple folk?" replied de Vielle, a man of exceptional courage. "You engage in usury and beat your journeymen unmercifully. How many times have they come to me in tears?"

Tomas struck him in the face and shouted, "That's none of your affair, sinner. And I'll need to settle accounts with them too. Now, prepare to die, but first tell me where you keep your ducats."

But Monsieur de Vielle would not tell. They searched the whole house after they had killed him.

It turned out that he was a poor man, possessing very little apart from birth and honor. And so they put his home to the torch.

The women's turn came another day. Seven were accused of witchcraft and burned at the stake. Two were noblewomen, the rest commoners.

On Saint Ambrose's Day, Mehoune the baker, now the leader of the mob, said that I had been in communication with the court of Ghent for many years and had campaigned against privileges for the town of Arras. He was the first to cry, "Jan does not love our town as much as he should!" Then others spoke. There was so much bitterness in them. . . . And the things I heard about myself!

Gentlemen, a person thinks he lives within the four walls of his home, apart from the world, well hidden from the eyes and ears of his neighbors. It isn't so! We all bear a variety of grudges in our hearts that we have thrust out of mind; but when the time comes, they gather together, every last little slight, forming something horrendous to behold. There were parts of my life I couldn't remember myself, but the mob remembered everything. I swear I have no idea why they wanted my head. What had I done to them? In Arras I had been like clay molded by Albert into his own image and likeness. I had served faithfully, certain of reward. And now they were shouting for me to be taken to the stake!

"Jan is so wise!" they cried. "Too wise to live in our town anymore. We want to have a pure and humble faith, we want to obey Heaven, and we do not want wiseacres who insult us with their fancy talk and clever ideas. Our hands are calloused from hard work, and we trust only our hands and the teachings of the Holy Church. Meanwhile, Jan spends days and years on disputations, and he exalts reason, which is Satan's altar."

I was prepared to die by the time Albert spoke up: "I will not say that everything Jan has done deserves applause. He has sinned grievously against the town for, despite his many years of study, he is still full of vacillation and doubt. When I tell you that ardent Christian hearts can move mountains, he immediately counters with his own view—the heart has no arms and legs with which to move anything. When I call out to you saying that desire is all, he does not conceal his doubt, arguing that intelligence also comes from God. It has been said here that reason is the devil's tool. That's not true! But it is true that the devil can dwell only in the mind and never in the heart of man. I would not be able to answer the question of whether or not Jan is guilty! His heresy lies mostly in his lack of trust, for all his fine efforts. He constantly yields to strange promptings. They might come from the devil, or his submission may just be out of weakness. We should be concerned with the salvation of this soul, not its damnation. I think Jan should be removed from the council so as to have time for meditation and prayer. Then we shall see. . . ."

As I walked from the chamber, I said loudly and clearly that I am true to the town of Arras and will remain true. Mehoune the baker burst into acerbic laughter. That was the last time I saw him, for the next day his life was taken by a man whose daughter he had seduced.

And so it was that I found myself in my own home, far from the doings of the town. I spent the following days in utter solitude, listening intently to scores being clamorously settled. Indeed I did devote myself to meditation. I was in an exceptionally painful position. At first glance, it might seem that Arras was expelling me: but in fact it was I who had expelled the town from my heart. Oh, I wasn't pained by the sentence the council had passed against me, for I had never attached any significance to what commoners thought. For a long time, however, Albert had struck me as obsessed. I did not truly suspect him of madness but rather sensed some hidden idea at work in him, one that he did not wish to reveal to others. And so I was not in the least aggrieved by my expulsion from the council. I even turned it to advantage! Over the last few days, I had been acting without conviction. If Arras wants to plunge to the lowest depths, I thought, let it do so without me. It's all to the good that I'm sitting at home, fairly isolated, and of course no longer able to have any influence on the course of events. It wasn't the council's sentence I loathed, but the council itself. I admit it was bitter to think that only after so long a time had I seen its true face, which did not speak well of my judgment.

A vulgar mind would no doubt think that danger helped me regain my judgment. As long as I was on top, I allowed myself to be misled along with the rest of the town; however, when I fell, I experienced a revelation. That would not be a sound opinion, gentlemen! Things were not so simple. There is, however, a grain of truth in that idea. That's how life nearly always is, and you shouldn't curse the wind for blowing to port. You know that better than I, being in such close touch with the sea.

What thinking person doesn't experience the separateness of individuality as his greatest suffering? The company of God, even if He is the best of all possible companions, causes us more anguish than joy. And that is because in fact we remain alone. The life of the hermit! I always held it in such disdain. A person must be devoid of all humanity to live his life far away from the world, in dense forests or on top of inaccessible mountains. Since living on roots and spring water is not what counts, what is the measure for a hermit's acts? I once heard of a hermit from Artois who lived there ages ago and preached the gospel to the wild beasts. I think he must have been out of his mind. At first he might even have thought that the wolves, foxes, and martens were listening closely to him and even attempting to follow the teachings of Scripture. But then the wolf's nature would have gained the upper hand, and the beast would have said good-heartedly, "Stop your sermons, good father, for we're hungry and must go off to the forest to kill a deer." And I think that later on the hermit must have started going into the forest with them. First he watched, then he ate, and finally he hunted with them. Having neither powerful fangs nor sharp claws, he became the cruelest killer of the whole wild pack, and only then could he become its leader.

Gentlemen, I had a younger brother who locked himself away with the Carthusians three decades ago. He did not see another human being for a very long time and communed only with his faith. He went utterly mad. I tell you there must be some limits to our thoughts and actions, and also to our love of God. Even if God did not exist at all and only represented our longing, that longing would have to find its measure between one human heart and another.

Sometimes in my life, I have had the feeling of emerging from a dark wood where I was like the moss, the leaves, or the weasel. In these woods I did not yet know that I existed. But after I had experienced self-knowledge, I began seeking a point of reference. And I asked, where is that point?

When a ship leaves Bruges on a distant voyage, the people gathered on deck know only that they are alone amidst the furious elements of the sea. They look over at their captain, every sailor putting more trust in him than in God. All it takes is one careless move for a person to fall overboard and be lost, doomed. They all know that, and for that reason they work together. They seize the oars together and unfurl the sails together. If one despairs, all he need do is look at his comrade's strong arms to regain his spirit. And when they sail by shoals and underwater rocks, he never takes his eyes from his captain's lips.

Oh, I've heard how hard life is on your ships: hideous vermin, vile food, brutal work, the overseers' whips, and anyone who mutinies is hung from the yardarm. These sailors curse their fate and sometimes conceive a hatred for their ship. Still, they're overwhelmed with fear at the thought of hitting rocks, being smashed to bits, and sinking to the bottom. Some have survived such incidents. They stayed alive on a tiny boat, a plaything of the sea, for long weeks on end. Alone between sky and water, they found it sweet to remember their ship, their comrades, their captain, and even their cruel overseers. On the ship, despite everything, they had been human beings; whereas now they were no more than toys of the raging elements. . . .

To be oneself means to be no one else, and that is all. But one can only be oneself when one is among others. For this reason, I sat on the council and remained in Arras.

Well, but that is only part of the truth. When I was removed, I realized that I was not without guilt. Jan, I said to myself, why didn't you defend Farias de Saxe? Because he was not deserving of defense, was my immediate answer. He didn't appreciate his life and so better that he lost it! But then another thought would vex me. If the others were in favor of executing Farias de Saxe, then I should have been opposed in order to retain my individuality. But the desire for unanimity, I replied to myself, seems stronger than the desire for truth, because we do not derive our sense of security from the truth, but from the community. Arras is what unites us for better and for worse. Apart from Arras, we possess nothing. What about our faith? I asked in alarm. Faith, I answered, is the seed, while Arras is the soil. Without it, the mocking wind would scatter our faith to others' fields, and we would become beggars by church gates that had been slammed shut.

Gentlemen! I am inwardly cool and calm now as I tell you of my thoughts from last autumn; but then I experienced desperate flights and falls. I flitted around the house like a moth around a torchlight and never knew a moment's peace. All my licentious thoughts left me; I no longer even desired women, though I could have had them, for in my house I had women servants at my beck and call. For several days and nights, I sought a way out of my situation; meanwhile, the town bled like an open wound. Confidants would come running to me bearing terrible tales. Things were entirely different now than they'd been during the plague. At that time, Arras had been fighting for its life; but this was no more than the settling of petty scores. Informers made the rounds of every street, listening to what people were saying. Then they'd run to the council, but things were going badly even at the council, where now all were scowling at each other like wolves. Tomas the wheelwright, who had looted Monsieur de Vielle's house, accused the council of having a secret agreement with David. At first he was derided, but he was quite a cunning man and won the support of the worst riffraff in the town. Thus, Albert gave him a place on the council so that he would have a voice in its deliberations.

That wheelwright had a good head on his shoulders. He said, "No, it's wrong for everyone to dispense justice as he sees fit. We have the council headed by the Reverend Father Albert for that. There's been enough robbery on the streets; enough throats have been cut. Anyone with a score to settle should come before the council." His words occasioned great joy, for decent people were afraid to poke their noses outside after nightfall. It was decided that Tomas the Lame would be in charge of restoring order. And he did indeed!

A friend came to him and said, "Tomas, my good friend, I have a bone to pick with Monsieur Astruc. He loaned me a ducat, but I don't want to pay it back. Can you do something about it?"

Tomas scratched his head and said, "Bring a charge against Monsieur Astruc."

"What should I charge him with?" asked the friend.

"We'll figure it out," replied Tomas. "Come see me this evening, and I'll tell you!"

A charge was drawn up against Monsieur Astruc for insulting the Holy Trinity. Astruc stuttered when he said his prayers, and all he could stammer out was "the Father and the Son" but always stopped before "the Holy Ghost" to catch his breath. He was so torpid that even as he was being burned at the stake, he still could barely stammer out the words "Holy Ghost."

One afternoon I was visited by Pierre de Moyes, a tried and true friend who still sat on the council. When we were alone, he said, "Jan, a charge has been brought against you, and you will be placed under arrest."

"That can't be!" I cried, seized with fear. "What does Albert have to say about it?"

"Albert has yielded to pressure from the council," said de Moyes.

"Who voted against the charge?" I asked my friend.

"No one," he replied, growing sad for a moment, but then added at once, "Which is why I wanted to inform you of the council's decision as quickly as possible."

He looked warily to every side as he left my house. He was a very honorable man, though faint of heart. Left alone, I at once regained my composure. So, they were all of one mind, with no idea of the wrong they were doing. They had relinquished their consciences to the herd like sheep, like a herd of damn goats. And it had not occurred to any of them that there was no more tyrannical tyranny in all the world than unanimity, no darkness darker than unanimity, no stupidity more stupid than unanimity! They had taken refuge in it, had placed the halter on their own necks. Oh, I suffered greatly on account of my isolation, but at the same time I was proud not to have had any part in all of that. It was then that I made my decision. I summoned a trusted servant and said to him, "Saddle my best horse and bring it to the Saint Aegidus' Gate. I'll be there before midnight."

The servant replied, "Sir, the guards are watching every thoroughfare."

"I know. I'll come armed. I don't have much to lose. If need be, I'll break through the guards and flee to Prince David."

"The town will bless your name!" he cried. "If only Prince David would come here, all this devilry would cease at once."

"I think so too," I said. "I won't stand calmly by while the heads of innocent citizens roll."

The servant left but returned at once. He said, "Sir, I fear for your life. If need be, I'll go with you, for I know how to use arms."

"I'll think about it," I said and dismissed the servant so that he would not see my tear-filled eyes. How glad I was at that moment to feel loved. And what of it that he was the very one who informed the council of my plan, as I was later to learn.

In the name of the Father, and of the Son, and of the Holy Ghost. Amen. I was greatly afraid. I was well aware of what was in store for a daredevil seized by the guards. The town of Arras is very cruel in that respect because it values the devotion of its citizens. The torture must last at the very least from sunup to sundown. I myself was among the authors of that law, which we proclaimed to the citizens in the year plague broke out. I took comfort in the thought that it was now late autumn. In midsummer the torture would be the most severe and last the longest. I realized I was taking a great risk, but I did not want to think of what would happen if I were seized.

I left the house before midnight, the most opportune hour. The night was dark, the sky covered with clouds, no sign of the moon and stars. The town was asleep, the only sound the distant communal prayer from the Church of the Holy Trinity. I pulled up my hood and wrapped myself in a cloak. I took a knife with me, very narrow and sharp with a handgrip, that could strike to the heart in a single thrust. I walked slowly so as not to attract attention. The servant was waiting for me near Saint Aegidus' Gate, which heartened me greatly, for I was counting on his help. I could not see his face in the dark but was glad that he was with me.

"Do you have a weapon?" I asked quietly.

"I do," he replied in a voice so faint it terrified me. I looked over at the gate and saw that it was wide open, and that the guards were playing dice. This had never happened before. Since the town of Arras was always shut tight at nightfall, to be opened again to all the world at sunrise, I had thought I would have to lower myself over the wall. For that purpose I had had the servant strap a strong hempen rope to the saddle. The moat had dried up quite some time ago from a lack of rain, leaving a nasty swamp around the walls, but one easy to cross, knee deep in mud. Once on the other side, I planned to open a secret gate made during the time of plague. The servant would bring me my horse there. The gate locked from the outside because the bishop had ordered it made for the use of the guards who at the time lived outside the walls surrounding the town.

I was intending to escape in that fashion when I had suddenly observed that the town gate was wide open. Then the servant whispered to me, "Sir, forgive my faintheartedness, but I've taken fright and won't be going with you."

"Why's that?" I said. "You're the one who offered help."

The servant replied, "I know, but my teeth chatter at the thought of what will happen if they catch us. They'll peel off our skin, cut off one limb after the other, yank out our tongues, gouge out our eyes, and then slowly . . ."

"Silence, you numskull!" I said, interrupting the wretch, the hair bristling on my head.

He fell silent. I looked over at the gate. A Cistercian monk was walking by, supporting himself with a staff. The guards didn't even glance at him although he was an outsider, for Cistercian monks had never lived in Arras. I thought that if he was a discerning man, he would inform Prince David of what was happening in our town. I said to the servant, "Take the horse back to the stable and get some sleep." Before I knew it, he was gone.

In the name of the Father, and of the Son, and of the Holy Ghost. Amen. I have already said that the town of Arras had played a devilish trick on me. How could I have just walked out through those open gates? It was one thing to surmount obstacles or to fight to the death with the guards, but just to walk out the gate? When passing sentence on me, the council had not been aware that Albert would wish to subject me to the cruel temptation of an open gate.

Back at home, I felt I'd made the right choice. If the town is mad, I shall be sober minded. If it is evil, I shall be good. Albert had wished to subjugate me by showing me trust. All right then, I thought with some emotion, I'll repay him in kind, though I know I'll have to suffer terribly for it later on. If Arras wants me to be a part of its destruction, I'll serve it as a rebuke to its conscience.

It's unbelievable, gentlemen, but I went to sleep that night, and slept well. I was woken by the sun when it was already high in the sky. My first thought was of the Cistercian monk whom I had seen on the bridge. If there is one drop of Christian love in him, he'll certainly go to Ghent, for is that not his duty? I also knew that the Cistercians did not like Albert because he always mocked them, while praising the Dominicans to the skies. This was understandable given the Reverend Father's tendency to preach and, also, the Cistercians' subordination to any bishop. And so I hoped that monk would go straight to Ghent. Feverishly, I calculated how much time would pass before Prince David appeared at the gates of Arras. This calculation did not prove overly comforting, for the guards could come for me at any minute.

And so I passed the day in anxiety, listening closely for footsteps in the courtyard and keeping an eye out for the approach of the guards. I kept sending my manservant outside to bring me news, but he would return, saying, "Not a soul in sight, sir, just a few pigs scratching themselves by the gate."

Finally, long after sunset, when the oil lamp was already dying out, there was some commotion at the entrance. The servant came running and said that the Reverend Father had come. I greeted him at the door. As he entered, he did not give me his hand to kiss but exclaimed that I did not love the town of Arras and its people in the least, which I denied.

Then he said, "You were about to flee to the bishop's court and bring David down on our backs!"

I denied it. He laughed. I could see that he was weak and looked very swollen. He suffered terribly from dropsy, which he had throughout his body and which grew worse each day. I invited him to stay awhile, called the servants, and ordered the finest drink brought.

"I don't want anything in this house!" he shouted angrily. Once again he said that I had intended to decamp from Arras.

"That's not true," I replied forcefully.

Then he summoned the servant whom I had sent to the gates with my horse. "Say what you reported to me yesterday morning!" he ordered. The servant admitted everything, gazing haughtily at me. And so it was that I realized I had been nurturing a serpent in my breast, one who had delivered me to ruination.

When Albert and I were alone, I said, "Father, hear me out! It's true I wanted to go to Prince David, for I can no longer bear to look upon these atrocities. It's time they're all done with! It's time for the town to live by its conscience again and show some contrition. . . ."

He was about to interrupt, but I kept on speaking, for I knew I was fighting for my life. "And that is why I intended to go to David, but, after all, I didn't go. I withdrew at the last minute for Arras is my town, and I don't wish to betray it, even for its own good!"

Albert laughed so coldly and cruelly that my legs buckled at the knees. "You're lying," he said, the words whistling from his mouth, saliva spraying onto his beard. "You're lying, Jan! You did not abandon your intention to flee out of love for Arras but out of sly cowardice. If your servant hadn't deserted you, you would have gone through the gate and done battle with the guard. They were waiting for you. For I was putting you to the test. But you outsmarted me. . . . You are intelligent, and you are abominable. You knew what to expect from the torturer if you were caught. Nothing could save you then."

Hope entered my heart when he said that. But it was quickly extinguished when he said, "You'll be beheaded! But you'll be spared torture."

I said, "Father! Don't do that to your most faithful pupil. What do you want from me and this town? What devil is driving you, and what do you hope to accomplish by burning people at the stake, by handing the best people over to be executed?"

He shouted and raised his hand as if to strike me, but then suddenly went slack and sank weakly down on a bench. I looked at him and understood nothing. Tears were streaming down his old cheeks, huge with dropsy, and falling onto his white beard. His whole body was shaking like a shrub in the wind. I clapped my hands, and when my manservant appeared, I ordered him to bring a jug of wine. "No need," said Albert softly, but he drank greedily. Once again he burst into tears.

I sat down by him. Hope throbbed in me like a hooded falcon, yet my heart was also filled with bitter sorrow. After all, he had been my protector and teacher for so many years, this worthiest and firmest of men on earth. For twenty years he had kept a tight rein on a great town, and here he was weeping like a child, unable to utter a word. I spoke softly: "Father Albert, don't worry. . . . Everything will be all right!" And I believed it would be. I began speaking to him as if consoling a child. I even had the urge to take his hand and kiss it when I suddenly remembered what was happening in this town and restrained myself.

Then he glanced at me from under his swollen eyelids, and I thought only a blind man's eyes could look at you like that. But he could see. "What do you think, Jan, that's it's easy for me here in this town?" he said softly. "That I have a heart of stone and my mind is afflicted with enmity for the human race? I suffer terribly, like no one else in Arras suffers!"

"What are you trying to do, Father?"

"To liberate them!" he replied with sudden force. "To bring them some light in this awful darkness." He was speaking more loudly now, and the

tears had dried on his face. But do not think, gentlemen, that he had been visited by inspiration or some
demonic spark. Nothing of the sort! Beneath the surface of his words was a singular clarity of mind that
weighed everything, connected everything, and illuminated everything to the fullest, which only made
his words all the more terrible. "Jan," he said to me,
"I wanted you to be my successor. I knew I would
never reach my goal. The road is very long and demands great rigor. Think of this unfortunate town,
and how it desired liberation! Men and women were
expelled from Paradise and do not feel this world is
theirs: it's alien to them, oppressive, evil, indolent.
They are born, and they die in a sorry whirl of actions,
shearing sheep, making rope, weaving serge. They
are born, and they die without knowing why they
came into this world. After all, it is not the purpose of
man to shear sheep, make rope, and weave serge. And
it is not man's purpose to sleep with women, eat, milk
cows, shoe horses, or hunt the beasts of the forest.
Where is the Paradise, lost to them even before they
came into the world, and where should it be sought
that some bit of meaning may be found in this mad-
house? A few years ago a terrible plague befell them.
They cut each other's throats and ate human flesh. A
true Hell! And when the plague died out, they once
again returned to their serge and ropes; they went to
seed, grew despondent, their hearts dried and shriv-
eled. When a fungus grows on the trunk of a mighty
tree, you need axes and strong arms to hack it off. Yet
sometimes even that's not enough, and a fiery light-

ning bolt from Heaven must strike and consume everything around it, topple the tree and turn it into a smoking pyre so that the following year a healthy seed may sprout at the site of the blaze.

"By the Western Gate where the Jews live, there is a small pond covered by duckweed and water lilies. In time that pond will become even more overgrown. When I was there years ago, the water was pure, and fat carp swam in its depths. As time passed, the duckweed spread from the bank, and the lilies covered the whole pond with a green scum of vegetation, voracious and insatiable. The carp floated to the surface, their gills swollen, and there was no life left in the pond, which pained me greatly. Why was there no light for those poor fish in the depths of the water? Did they have to die out with no hope at all? I went there several times and threw stones into the depths of the water. All the green scum covering the pond distended furiously, and a movement of some sort ran across the surface; the duckweed trembled, the water lilies closed and flattened, and a column of pure water gushed from the depths. At one point I hired people to throw stones along with me. They thought I was out of my mind. Not everyone can understand love. And so what had happened to the pond? It had become like the jaws of Hell. I wanted to burn off those lilies and growths to clear the surface of the water and let in the sunlight. When people threw stones, something began to stir in the depths, and the water came back to life, as if the pond had finally reawakened. I ordered people to lash the lilies with birch rods, which they did. Those lilies writhed in pain, went into terrible convulsions, and where the blows fell, the pure water shone through.

"Jan, trust me. I swear that this town must be flogged till it bleeds, burned from every quarter, turned into the dwelling place of the beast, so that the true face of man may be revealed. People here wanted nothing more than change! They wanted it even at the cost of terrible pain, because everything in their lives was empty, flat, fetid, torpid, rotten, and insipid. Lick mist and what do you taste? Nothingness. All Arras was one great tongue licking mist. People even died without regret and fear, so empty had they grown. Oh, you're sorely mistaken if you think I wanted to make angels of those people. I only wanted them to be more human than they had been. Jan, my son, tell me, when can a person know the sweetness of virtue? When he has known the bitterness of sin! When can he fully fathom the meaning of peace? When he knows the meaning of anxiety and fear! When can a person thirst for God? When he has tasted of the devil! When can a person begin to love life as it is? When he has had a brush with death! When can a person appreciate food, clothing, horses, the udders of a cow, the beauty of textiles, and the delicate feel of serge? When he has been consumed night and day by despair, pain, and the greatest fear! When can a person finally recognize that certain values are enduring? When he has hit the lowest depths, where nothing endures and nothing has value. And that is my way of leading this town to true freedom."

He fell silent. I looked at him and thought he had gone mad. But he guessed that. "You think I've gone mad, don't you? All right, then show me another way, a better way, one more worthy of human beings. People have experienced unspeakable suffering since the dawn of time. Prophets come to them and say, 'Follow me and I will bring you into Paradise!' And people humbly follow them, for man wants nothing more than to be on the move; it doesn't matter where, as long as he is going somewhere. Trust me, my pupil! There is nothing more difficult than winning God's favor. People have been in pursuit of God since time immemorial, constantly advancing over innumerable corpses and cripples, amid deafening battle cries, slaughter, murder, and conflagration. They are indefatigable in that great longing of theirs. And anyone who wishes to halt them does evil, for we are destined to move forward, and only then do people feel free."

"Free!" I said mockingly, forgetting that I was in danger. "What is the freedom you have given the town of Arras? It is the cruelest of all slaveries—of violence, accusation, the stake, spells, and pathetic delusion."

He smiled at my words and said, "Jan, it doesn't matter what things are, but what they're called. The name is all. When God revealed Himself to Moses on Mount Horeb, Moses asked, 'Lord, what is Thy name?' And God answered, 'I am that I am!' You speak of the slavery of violence and delusion into which the town has fallen. You are mistaken! What is violence that is called 'punishment'? It is punishment. And what is a delusion that is called 'belief in salvation'? It is the belief in salvation! You think man is made of acts and intentions, but he is also made of words. You are not the first to succumb to the most foolish illusion of the human mind—that the world can be known and changed without words. How can you know and change it without the language that was given you to name the things of the world? What has no name does not exist. And what does exist, exists because of its name."

Then, stirred to my depths, I cried out, "Father Albert, the devil is speaking through your lips!"

Once again, he laughed quietly. "So you've given it a name, have you, Jan! You've learned language and are now using it. You say it's the devil! Turn your head a little and give it another name, and you'll hear something different. You say 'I' and saying that sets you apart; but when you say 'we,' that makes you a part. I'm telling you that when you say 'I,' you sin; and since I say so, it is so! Thus, I've given a name to what you say, just as I have given a name to all the acts committed by this town. And they are what this name says they are. What's happening now in Arras I call 'freedom,' and others have followed my example and called it 'freedom' too—and so it is freedom and nothing but freedom. I forced the town to do what it is doing, but it wants to do what it must do. If you don't see this as harmony and the only path to salvation, you are deaf, dumb, and blind. I am assuming the burden of all the town's sins and am ready to suffer for them as no one has suffered before. I forced them to obey my orders, and in obeying them, they discovered their own free will and joy. If that isn't freedom, nothing is. And, finally, can you tell me who loves this town more than I do? I would condemn myself to eternal damnation if only Arras could know the pleasure of calling things and actions by their right name."

He rose and looked triumphantly at me. Still, I said, "Father, forgive me! But I have heard you say terrible things that will undoubtedly lead everyone here to their doom."

Smiling again, he spoke: "Even so, what of it? When a person stands still, he starts to fear death. But when he's on the move, he even forgets that he must die. Arras is on the move, Jan! Everyone here will die with a light heart. Even you!" I began to quake. "Don't worry," he said. "I'm leaving now. The town guard will come for you at dawn. You will be placed under arrest and will have to face the council. I'll tell you right now you're already condemned to death, but you will die an easy death, without suffering, because you are the person I love best in Arras. But you wished to stop the town's march, and for that you must be punished."

Having said this, he left my house. I grabbed the jug of wine, drained it avidly, then smashed it against the wall and wept in fear of death.

In the name of the Father, and of the Son, and of the Holy Ghost. Amen. Gentlemen, citizens of the excellent city of Bruges who have shown me such hospitality! Judge for yourselves—was not the Reverend Father a very wise man? It's all a matter of names! No being can exist without a name. I am who Jan is, and for that reason, I exist. But if I were to say to you that the city of Bruges sows fish, and you accepted what I said; then all the citizens of Bruges would walk into the sea with sickles to harvest fish. Many people would drown, but, after all, a goodly number would return to shore carrying baskets full of threshed fish. Whole families would walk out into the sea, just as they go out to the fields, and mow the foamy waves with their sickles. But any ship sailing by would unfailingly be dashed on the rocks because all the sailors on board would lose their minds at the sight of you. I am, however, most stirred by the thought that there would be worthy and respected people in Bruges, fathers of families and serious businessmen, who would find pride and joy in those sea harvests and sharpen their sickles every night to go out again the next dawn to harvest fish. And anyone who said that the proper thing to do was use a net would undoubtedly be driven from the city for spreading disbelief and fear.

Gentlemen, be mindful of what your own worthy council has to say, for the day may come when fish begin to sing in Bruges, birds are caught with fishing rods, stallions milked, and cows saddled: for things are not what they are, but what they are called! I can feel my throat clutch with fear as I speak these words.

And so, the guards came for me that same evening. I offered no resistance and said to the leader, "Wait by the door while I put on some warm clothing; it's very cold in the dungeon."

He replied, "That's true. And bring along a demijohn of wine; the guards like to drink and play dice
with the prisoners and have a good time with them."
I did as he advised. They took me through a good
portion of the city on the way to the town hall. People
could see my plight, but they showed me no sympathy. Mostly, they seemed weary, as if the fire that had
consumed the town were slowly dying out. That was
comforting.

I was locked in a dungeon I knew well since for
many years I had directed the building of the town
hall. The cell was dark and damp, but I found a
bench there and a bit of straw. I was not chained to
the wall, for I had not yet been found guilty and was
only waiting to be brought before the council. On
the whole, I must admit that the guards treated me
decently and with a certain respect. Father Albert
had clearly ordered that no great harm be done me.
Night fell, and the guards lit some resinous chips to
provide light. One of them said, "Good sir, will you
play dice with us?"

"With great pleasure," I replied. And so we
played dice until the clock on the tower struck midnight. Then I lay down on the bench and fell asleep. I
was in a strange state, for while I was aware of death
approaching, I did not lose my peace of mind or even
a certain good cheer. I suspected this was a form of
madness, as if, despite myself, I had taken refuge in
insanity against the thought of my terrible end. In any
case, I had not cried again since I had burst into tears
after Albert had left, and I even felt merry at times. As

I was playing dice with the guards, I had a great desire to win, so much so that every bad roll angered me, while I burst out laughing with every lucky throw. As I was falling asleep, I heard one guard say, "He's a truly great man, he doesn't fear death."

Thus I passed two peaceful days in the dungeon, days that even now I recall without regret. Then one of the guards came to me for a sip of wine. He slipped into the cell and said softly, "Good sir, prepare to die. I know what you'll be accused of."

"So tell me then!" I said to him.

"The whole town knows that you were in league with the Count de Saxe, working to reduce Arras's privileges. When you came to speak with him in his cell before his execution, he gave you letters for Prince David and Prince Philip."

"How could he give me letters when he was in a dark cell without paper or pen?" I cried in reply.

But the guard said, "That I don't know. But there's no doubt he gave you letters for Prince David."

"So then where are they now? Proof should be presented."

"I heard in town that the letters got lost," replied the guard. "And no one knows where they are now. But everyone knows that the Count de Saxe wrote the letters, and that you hid them to give to the bishop later."

"How can you know that?" I shouted in despair. "Think about it, man! Can a person write letters in a cell like this?"

He replied calmly, "I don't know how to write! And so I don't know how it's done. But the count did write, and you hid the letters."

My reply was, "You're nothing but a horse. Get up on your hind legs and neigh!" He looked at me as if he hadn't understood. So I repeated it: "I say, get up on your hind legs and neigh, because you're nothing but a horse."

"I'm not a horse," he said.

"You're wrong," I cried in anger. "The whole town knows you're a horse. Monsieur de Moyes broke you in and bought a fine saddle for you. But you were ornery, and so you were harnessed with another horse to a cart for hauling serge."

"I'm not a horse," he stammered.

To which I replied firmly, "Prove it!" He ran from my cell. I think that when he found himself on the street in front of the town hall, he must have neighed and galloped straight to the blacksmith.

And that was how I found out what the council had in store for me. There was no hope for me; I had to prepare for my death. Yet I took comfort in the thought that I would be spared torture. Evidently, Albert had concealed from the council my plan to escape during the night. I praised myself for the prudence I had shown at the time. It was a good thing I had withdrawn from Saint Aegidus' Gate. They were just waiting for me to emerge from the shadows and take a step toward the wall. They would have had me then! I would have suffered indescribable agonies from sunup to sundown.

Once again, some time passed. I had no idea whether it was dawn, day, twilight, or night. In my cell it was always dark and dank. I would ask the guards what time of day it was, and they would answer me politely. Finally, a boy named Sol, who had been my servant before I sent him to work at the town hall, came to me and said, "Good sir, I've brought you a very tasty supper because tonight you go before the council and at sunrise to the executioner. Since it's your last night, I'll go to pray for you right now." He left me a lavish meal. Later I learned that my servants had prepared the meal, unquestionably a great proof of their love and courage since similar gestures had cost other people their heads in Arras.

So, I called the guards, and we ate together. There was an exquisite pie, a very delicately prepared smoked pork rump, and fieldfare as well. We also had a demijohn of wine and a jug of beer. While eating, I said to the guards, "And so, good people, tomorrow at sunrise I'll be going to God."

"It's Heaven's will," said one.

I replied, "But I think there might be some trouble because Arras's executioner has been killed. Who'll cut off my head?"

The same man said, "There won't be any trouble, because I was at the council today and I made a humble request: I said that I'd cut off my lord's head."

I almost choked on my pie when he said that. "And so you're going to do it?"

"Yes, me, sir!"

"Show me your arm." He got up from the ground

and threw off his shirt, baring himself to the waist. He truly was a fine specimen. I touched the powerful knots of muscle taut under his skin, and a shudder ran through me. Then I said, "Why did you ask to be allowed to do it? Do you know me?"

"No, I don't, good sir, but the council's paying three ducats for your head."

"Three ducats," I said pensively. "I didn't think I was worth all that much."

There was still a good deal of food left, but I had lost my appetite. Whenever I looked at that man's arms, a shudder went through me. They drank all the beer, then finally left, taking their torch with them. I was enveloped in total darkness. I sat down, leaned back against the cold wall, and listened to the beating of my heart.

In the name of the Father, and of the Son, and of the Holy Ghost. Amen. I admit that I was terribly afraid to die, for I am a very sinful man. Yet there was something soothing about the darkness and the stillness, as if I didn't exist or existed apart from the world and people. I could hear my heart thumping, my breath whistling. I touched my body avidly with the palm of my hand. Nothing existed apart from me. I filled the whole world with myself. If death is only this, then it does not seem so cruel. . . . I remained in that state of contemplation, desiring one thing only—never again to see faces, trees, the sky, and the sun. Were I to be killed in that cell, in the basement of the town hall, in darkness and utter stillness, I would have been granted a gentle extinction. And, thinking that, I understood all the cruelty of prison and execution.

I was in a strangely listless state broken by bursts of desperate thought. Perhaps I had fallen asleep; perhaps I kept waking up; but something was holding me perfectly still, and I did not want to break that spell. You might say I was giving myself some training in dying.

Then I heard some noise, followed by a flaring glow at the far end of the dungeon. I decided to face the end manfully. They were coming for me now to drag me in front of the council and from there, at daybreak, to the block. I did not want to have eyes, ears, a tongue, a sense of smell, or touch. Yet I had them, and to such hideous excess that it was impossible to describe in words.

The torchlight was brighter now. The footfall was closer. I rose slowly to my feet. The man who was to behead me now stood before me. "Good sir!" he cried. "Prince David, bishop of Utrecht, has entered the town through Trinity Gate!" And he fell to his knees. "Forgive me that I was tempted by three ducats, but I'm a very poor man. . . ."

"Hold up the torch; it's going out!" I said, rebuffing him. "Bring me to the bishop at once."

And that is how I was saved by a miracle, gentlemen! It was like some parable of evil dragons and virtuous knights. Just as a terrible sword rises to lop off the head, a supernatural force stops it midway, and the good Lord rewards the condemned man for his faith and suffering. As I hastened down the under-

ground corridor, preceded by the would-be executioner with the torch, I experienced a moment of great
singularity. I was so overwhelmed by joyous surprise
that I was ready to believe that my demeanor had
won me a miracle from God. But even if my mind does
sometimes fall into such pits, it's never for long! I was
back to my senses by the time I was outside and in the
town hall courtyard. The night was cool, but it had
been so bitterly cold in the dungeon that I had nothing whatsoever to complain of now. A mob was gathered in the courtyard, along with a few lords who
greeted me courteously, and even, I would say, ob-
sequiously. All Arras knew I was the bishop's friend.

There was no one from the council about; they
had all gone to the Trinity Gate. Torchlight lit the
faces in the crowd, but I glimpsed no relief there, no
fear, no joy. The faces looked sleepy. It was only then
that I realized it was approaching midnight, and I had
thus been saved only a few hours before the end.

David rode into the town hall courtyard on
horseback, led by the council, which maintained its
silence. I saw Albert, barely able to walk, supported
by others. Catching sight of me, the bishop halted his
horse and cried, "Jan! I'm so glad to see you." Then he
spoke with pity of how badly I looked. I went inside
the town hall with him while the others waited outside the door.

My first words to him were, "Your Majesty, you
arrived just in time. They were going to behead me at
daybreak."

"But you're safe and sound now," he replied,

taking me by the arm. "Now tell me everything that's happened in Arras."

Gentlemen, what was I to say to him? Is it possible to summarize so much suffering in a few words? How to begin, where to end? Suddenly it occurred to me that to explain in the fairest way what had happened here, I should begin with the creation of the world. "Forgive me, Prince, but I am too weary to tell you. It was just a short while ago that I was in the town hall's dungeon, preparing myself for death. Let me go now, and I'll come back later."

"You're right," said David. "Go rest. And when you feel strong enough, I'll be glad to see you, as always."

And so I left the bishop's chambers and found myself in the courtyard again. It was deserted now. Everyone had returned home, as if nothing unusual had happened that night. And, truly, nothing had changed! It was just that I had experienced my own resurrection. I was very weary and sleepy, but I took myself in hand and went looking for the man who was to have been my executioner. I lay in wait for him in the guards' room. When I saw him, I said, "You were supposed to get three ducats for my head. Here's three ducats for you." I removed a beautiful ring from my finger. He refused, smelling a trick, so I said, "Don't be afraid. Take the ring. I want you to enjoy life as I am enjoying it. And pray for me." Then he took the ring and kissed my hand.

I left the town hall for home, but I walked very, very slowly. Night was already receding. The black

and starless sky was changing and had begun to re-
semble poorly laundered serge, delicately specked
with water stains, or a soundlessly rent curtain. I was
troubled. At that moment I was to have been escorted
from the council hall to the gates of the Church of the
Holy Trinity. The guards would have slowed their
step, keeping a close watch on the sky. "Not yet . . .
Stop!" they'd say. A wind had sprung up and begun to
blow through the bare treetops. Along with it came
the smell of the damp meadows that began right outside the city walls. Once again the guards would lead
me on. In the east the sky was more deeply rent. A
rooster began to crow. Hoofbeats clattered somewhere on the frozen ground. And now the Church of
the Holy Trinity emerged from the darkness, now the
cold pierced me to my marrow. But why are there no
torches inside the church? Why is there no singing?
The bishop has arrived, and so no torches have been
lit for me, no psalms sung to bid me farewell. All
thanks to you, Prince! Then came the first ray of sun,
still beneath the rooftops, something more felt than
seen. I passed the scaffold. I could see the block on
top. During the day it was rust red from blood, but at
this hour it was a black, squat silhouette.

I was at my door as pink rays slanted across the
roof of my house. At that moment my head would
have been rolling. I touched it tenderly. It sat firm on
my neck.

I entered the hall, then went through the courtyard to the servants' quarters. I knew they had stayed
home, for I had been too generous for them to have

wanted to observe their master's death. When they saw me in the doorway, they fell to their knees in terror, thinking my ghost had returned home. But they soon understood that I was alive and enjoying my freedom, and they raised a joyous lament. I, however, was looking only for one of them. Then I saw him. He understood what lay in store for him and was about to flee, but was prevented. I said, "You all know that it was he who consigned me to death. Like Judas! He disgusts me. I will not lay a hand on him, but you do with him as you please." I walked out of the servants' quarters. On my way back to my chambers, a terrible cry reached my ear, followed by a second, and a third. . . . Then all was still.

A while later my footman crept into my bedroom to attend me before I went to bed. I could see that the palms of his hands were red with blood. "Wash yourself," I said. "And don't touch my clothing." He left and I went to bed.

Thus ended the terrible night of my death.

In the name of the Father, and of the Son, and of the Holy Ghost. Amen.

The next afternoon Chastell brought me news that the Reverend Father Albert had taken ill and very much wished to see me. I didn't want to go, but Chastell added that this was also the bishop's will. And so I went to Albert's house. A Dominican from Ghent, who had come to Arras with the bishop, was with him and was just hearing the Reverend Father's confession. I waited in the next chamber by the door, which was ajar. I could hear muffled whispers, which went

on for a very long time. Finally, the Dominican came
to the door, covering his nose with the sleeve of his
habit. "The old man reeks," he muttered and left. I
entered the dying man's room. Albert glanced at me,
and I at him. It was clear that these were his last
minutes of life. And he did indeed smell terrible. I sat
down by his bed and said not a word. He motioned me
to lean closer to him. He was so swollen from within
that he could barely speak, and it cost him great effort
to move his tongue.

He whispered, "Jan, my pupil, I'm dying now. I
have accepted God in my heart and am in good spir-
its. I have been forgiven my trespasses; so I summoned you to tell you that I too forgive."

"What do you forgive, Father?" I asked in great
amazement.

"I always told you, Jan, that I am Arras and Arras
is me. And it'll be that way as long as I'm alive. And so
I forgive your trespasses against Arras. And tell the
other citizens that I forgive them too for their trespasses against the town. They did not keep faith with
it to the end, and they will yet have to pay for that, but
I forgive." I said nothing for I had been seized by a
sudden anger at the old man. "Not everything people
believe is pleasing to God. But any faith is better than
none. Some people in Arras thought they should follow the example of the princes and bishops, and devote their minds to higher philosophy and knowledge
of the world. Meanwhile, first and foremost, their task
was to have faith. . . ."

"Father Albert," I interrupted without hiding the mockery in my voice. "What kind of faith can those on the bottom and those on top have in common? Those who judge and those who are judged?"

He tried to close his eyes, but his eyelids were so swollen that I could still see his pupils. He made no reply. It seemed that at the end, in the last minutes of his life, he finally understood that he was not speaking to the person to whom he thought he was or wished he were. . . .

Oh, gentlemen, how he must have suffered when he understood that! He had spent so many years trying to fashion me in his image and likeness, and to bequeath his entire legacy to me. Then suddenly, at the hour of his death, he realized he had lodged all those hopes in vain. I knew that caused him pain, but was I to deceive him in the sight of God? Was I to make believe like some wretched actor? No! That I could not do. Certainly, I had compassion for Albert, but was I not myself deserving of compassion and, above all, of the concern that is better shown to the living than to the dead?

Our paths had diverged, not when I sat at the old man's bedside, but many years earlier. We both knew that. It was just that he had attempted to preserve his illusions, and I had not!

Albert no longer spoke but only gazed from under his swollen eyelids. His eyes were like stone that turned me to stone. But I bore his gaze for quite a long time, then quietly left the room.

He died that day, and those who were with him until the end said later that his last words were: "Believe and endure!"

That same day the bishop summoned me and asked if I had spoken to Albert as he lay dying. He seemed very curious and unable to conceal it. And so I said to David, "Yes, Your Majesty, we spoke, on the subject of faith."

He burst into derisive laughter. "I can just see the two of you chatting about faith. But, dear Jan, tell me the whole truth! Was I mentioned?"

"No, Your Majesty."

He looked me straight in the eye and said, "Jan, this is very important to me, so tell the truth."

I replied, "Prince, I would never dare lie to you. Believe me, you were not mentioned in that conversation; there was not a single word about you. For better or worse, nothing was said of you!"

He furrowed his brow as if he were somewhat disappointed. At the time I thought he had a great desire to have been spoken of by the dying man. That would be of some value to a person like David, though I swear I could never understand that sort of weakness.

In the name of the Father, and of the Son, and of the Holy Ghost. Amen.

Gentlemen, now I shall summarize for you what happened after the bishop's arrival in Arras and the Reverend Father's death. Unusual events took place for several days, but the most important day was the Sunday that came to be known as the Sunday of Forgiveness, Cancellation, and Forgetting. And so I shall speak of that important day and everything that resulted from it. And with that I will conclude my confessions.

Preparations began that Sunday at daybreak. It was a windy but clear day, a common occurrence in late autumn. Small clouds shot through with sunlight raced across the sky. There was a coolness to the air, very brisk and bracing. Garlands of dried flowers somehow appeared in every home, their leafless branches cut from the foot of the town's walls, as did even a great deal of sweet flag and sinuous water lilies, which hung down like rats' tails. There was great animation among the Jews who had survived. The elder ordered that a fresh coat of whitewash be given to the streets leading to the Western Gate through which the bishop was to pass. The bishop had announced he would visit the Jewish community, probably the first time this had ever happened. The doors of Saint Aegidus' Church were wide open, and the altar glowed with innumerable resinous chips. The smoke so filled your nostrils that you couldn't get your breath. Standards with the coats of arms of all our good princes blossomed on the walls. There was the standard of Prince Philip and Prince David, and also that of King Louis, the new ruler in Paris. While we had been grappling with conscience in Arras, God had summoned King Charles. His worthy son, who had been so hated by his father that he had to place himself under Burgundy's protection and endure many years at the court of Brussels, finally returned to French soil accompanied by a great retinue belonging to Prince Philip, who paid homage to him at the gates of Paris and offered him friendship and service on behalf of all Burgundy.

Arras looked sumptuous bedecked with greenery and standards, all the people in their best clothing. The bells were rung in all the churches while the enormous oxen, lambs, and fowl that David had bestowed upon the town were roasted in the streets. But I must confess I saw no joyful or happy faces. Once again the great wagon was back in its old familiar ruts, creaking its way forward, not knowing where it was going or why, and all that was certain was that it was heading for the next abyss fate had in store. The citizens of Arras took great care in welcoming the bishop and his court; and there were even those who expected changes for the better to come of this visit, but most were simply observing the good customs of the town.

I remember that when David came to Arras after the great plague and hunger, people welcomed him without any great outpouring of feeling but still with a certain degree of hope. During the famous banquet when he castigated us for the great pride we took in our recent sufferings, everyone was grateful to him and took delight in his person; but those times had long since passed. Moreover, in the plague year all Arras's citizens understood that God Himself or the devil had sent down that grievous fate upon us. The plague was not our doing, whereas we ourselves were accountable for the recent events that had claimed the lives of so many of our most worthy citizens. To be sure, here and there voices were raised saying some terrible illness must have seized Arras and disturbed the minds of its citizens, but most people paid that no heed. "We've searched enough for the causes of our suffering and for the evil that befell the town. One time it was the plague, another time it was God's will or the devil's tricks, or some mysterious disease. We're tired of all that and inclined to think that we are such as we are, meaning defective and foolish, quick to yield to the sweetness of empty words and the cruelty of cunning deceit. The town of Arras has no future! It will fade away, abandoned by God, the devil, and even by its princes, left to the mercy of its own powerlessness and the most insipid faith that ever lodged in the human heart. We are doomed, but we accept that sentence calmly, ready to go on living in accordance with our fate, to weave tapestries, trade in serge, and raise fat Picard bulls; but that does not signify in the least that we will ever find joy in our existence or rid ourselves of the fear of our own nature. Once again there shall come a day when we'll begin to cut each other's throats."

Outwardly, the town was festive, but people's hearts were filled with sorrow and fear.

That Sunday at noon David rode on horseback to the market. The horse was bay, the saddle and harness silver, and the plume on its head violet. The bishop stood in the stirrups while the horse pawed the ground with one hoof. This lasted for some time, with all the people gathered there humbly on their knees. Then David began to dismount, but his foot caught in the stirrup. He struggled furiously; a soldier ran over and helped him. Some people took this as a bad sign, but most people no longer believed in signs of any kind. The bells rang loudly, and loudest of all was the bell of Saint Fiacre's Church, the same one that had portended disaster before. The bishop entered the church, making the sign of the cross over the people. When he vanished inside, his horse began neighing vigorously, its nostrils, painted red, distended and covered with froth. Now some people said this was a good sign, while others were worried and remained silent.

Then a great mass began at Saint Aegidus' Church and lasted some five hours. Psalms and all the prayers were sung. The people wept much, and tears streamed from the eyes of many; yet I think their hearts remained cool. Even when Prince David, bishop of Utrecht, appeared by the vestibule with the Holy Sacrament, his arms linked with those of worthy fathers from Ghent, this did not make much of an impression on the citizens of Arras. How many times had they beheld the Sacrament, how many times had they accepted Christ, offering up all their faith to Him? And what had come of it?

Finally, the big moment came. David absolved the town of its sins and gave it his blessing. And he rendered all the trials null and void, as begun in bad faith, blasphemous, and nefarious. By virtue of his power as bishop, he struck down the trials of the Jew Itzak and the elder of the Jews, the trials of Monsieur de Saxe and Monsieur du Losch, the trial of the town executioner, and all the trials for witchcraft. "What has happened, never happened, and what was, never was!" Once again he blessed the town, beseeching God to absolve it of its sins and to expunge all its guilt.

The bells rang so loudly that an entire flock of birds flew over Arras in indescribable fright. Sweat ran into the eyes of the bell ringers, but David had paid them lavishly, and so they strained themselves to the limit. Blood trickled from their palms, and one of them fell from the tower and broke his bones.

The sun had already set when the bishop, again dressed in knightly garb, a hat on his head, wearing a cloak of violet and silver, rode on horseback toward the Western Gate, where he was welcomed by an assembly of officials of the Jewish community, who bowed low to him. A great wailing rose to the sky when the elder kissed the prince's hand. David said, "Live in this town in peace and plenty. I take you under my protection as are all the other citizens here!"

That evening the Prince ordered the town to make merry. Never before had so many torches burned in Arras. As noted by the worthy Monsieur Rolin who, despite his advanced years, had come from Brussels to observe the festivities, some thirty oxen, a hundred lambs, and fowl beyond counting were consumed that night. Barrels of beer and wine were constantly rolled out.

The prince feasted at the town hall, along with his court and a group of local lords. Once again we were in the same hall in which we had been three years before, and once again the citizens of Arras ate little while the court displayed no restraint. This time, however, David did not rebuke us. He seemed sad himself and did not even seem cheered by Albert's absence, his sworn enemy now finally gone forever.

The prince sat between myself and Chastell.

Gentlemen, that was indeed comical. How many times had I feasted in such company at the court of Ghent? After all, I was a close friend of David's, and more than once he had given me his women or loaned me falcons. As for Chastell, he was the guide and guardian of my youth; and what there is in me of the eagle or the bull I owe to him, while what I have of the fish or snake I ascribe to Albert; yet we were completely estranged from one another during that final feast. At one point, while drinking to my health, David said, "I know you're not happy, Jan. But I'm not happy either. None of us is." His eyes were very weary, like an ox after plowing. His entire face had assumed a tender expression, and there was something woman-ish about it, which struck me as unpleasant on that face, usually so hard and mocking. Chastell, the old-est of us and, I think, the wisest, nodded his head. That splendid tippler and carouser, renowned throughout Burgundy for decades, now looked like a rotted tree stump or, even worse, like a vesicle full of holes. All his strength was gone, and all he had left were the same old delusions.

Before I speak of the feast, I will mention what happened in the town when the bishop rode up to

Arras and ordered the gates opened. I know this from what I was told by various people, for, as you are aware, at the time I was in the cellars of the town hall preparing to die.

In the middle of the night, Albert, who had been attending prayers, was informed that an emissary of the bishop of Utrecht had arrived and demanded that all the town's gates be opened. Albert summoned the council as quickly as he could. Dragged from their warm beds, they gathered at the town hall. Pierre de Moyes told me that they looked more like straw men than living beings. Every face was puffy with fatigue and inner tension; their eyes were bloodshot, their limbs slack and devoid of strength. They sank heavily down on the benches and said not a word. Albert, then close to death and terribly swollen with dropsy, said, "David is coming to Arras and has ordered us to open the gates. His messengers are waiting by Trinity Gate. David himself is still an hour away from Arras but traveling at a swift pace. Councillors, what should we do?" The councillors remained silent. Then Albert added, "We cannot take up arms against the bishop, for that would be the most grievous of sins. And I will also tell you that we could not withstand attack."

If de Moyes was not lying and everything was as he said, then the council deserves a bow. No one cursed and no one wept. Calm prevailed among them. They regarded each other in silence. "Now it's our time to die!" said Tomas the wheelwright earnestly. Yvonnet the clothier nodded his silent assent. They were very pale and for a moment seemed to stand stock-still. Perhaps they were waiting for a miracle, but nothing happened.

I regret that I wasn't there to see them. Pierre de Moyes described it all in the following way: "You could hear the town hall's caretaker making some noise down by the henhouse. A bird cackled, and then all was still again. It was clear that the caretaker had grabbed a hen and then shoved it back in. Tomas the Lame said, 'Councillors, get ready to put your heads on the block!' The others still remained silent.

"Then Albert said, 'Let us pray for God's mercy.'

"To this Tomas replied quite calmly, 'Albert, there is no God who would forgive us.'

"The Reverend Father then said, 'God is one and everywhere the same.'

"Yvonnet interjected, 'We've had enough of your teachings, Father. They don't make us happy anymore.' But he said this calmly, without rancor.

"They all sat there in silence for a time, preparing themselves for death. It's incredible how much dignity they had and to what degree they were reconciled to their fate. Then there was some commotion outside, and the caretaker came into the council hall and said, 'The people by Trinity Gate report that the bishop is arriving. They don't know what to do.'

"Albert raised his eyes and looked at each councillor in turn and said, 'Citizens, come to a decision; it's time now!'

"Tomas was the first to rise. All eyes were on him

though everyone knew what he would say. Tomas touched his Adam's apple with the palm of his hand, closed his eyes, and said, 'We must open the gates to the bishop!'

"Yvonnet was next to speak. 'Let us open the gates,' he said. 'And let us go and pay our respects to the bishop as is only proper.' Others said the same. When my turn came, I could not utter a sound and so only nodded my head.

"Then Tomas said softly and with great calm, 'Monsieur de Moyes, speak your piece as the others have. You always were closemouthed, but now you too face the same dangers, the lash or exile, whatever God wills, and so speak up!' I nodded again and said that the gates must be opened. Then the caretaker ran from the chamber, and, led by Albert, we all followed him.

"Unaware of its fate, the town slept in innocence. I supported Albert by his right arm, and the cooper Nort took his left. The Reverend Father could barely shuffle along, he was so weak and heavy from all the water in him. We walked in silence, each of us thinking of only one thing. I did not notice anyone praying.

"A few guards had gathered at the gate, and all were in a state of fear. From the other side of the wall came the sound of many armed men on the move, the snorting of horses, impatient cries. I climbed a turret and looked down. And what I saw made my head spin. Torches burned along the walls as far as the eye could see, and in their glow I could make out a great throng of knights in armor on horseback. Where the torches were most concentrated, I saw Prince David on a bay charger. David wore no armor, only a cape and a cap. By the time I went down, Trinity Gate had been opened. Lit by a single torch, the council stood in silence. We heard the clang of iron as the guard opened the first gate. This was followed by the protracted creaking of chains as the bridge was slowly lowered. I glanced over at Yvonnet the clothier, who was closest to me, and saw two tears running down his face, but did not hear him moan.

"I was seized by alarm and was about to fall to my knees but remained motionless because the others were still standing. There was a commotion on the other side of the wall: the horses were rearing and snorting loudly as the prince's men made way for him. The prince was the first on the bridge; soldiers bearing torches flanked his horse. David was followed by his personal guard, but there were so many of them that a goodly portion remained outside the wall. Prince David halted his horse and dismounted. None of the council members knelt; we only bowed our heads. I was again supporting Albert by the arm, for he was not able to stand on his feet without help.

" 'Why doesn't the council welcome me?' said David softly. 'I'm arriving at night, probably not the best time, but I am very road weary and don't intend to wait long to be welcomed.'

"Then Tomas stepped forward, bowed still lower, and said clearly, 'The town of Arras welcomes you, Your Majesty Prince David, bishop of Utrecht, and commits itself to your care!'

"David took one step toward him and said, 'Who are you?'

" 'I am Tomas the wheelwright, known as the Lame because of my bad leg. I am a member of the council of the good town of Arras.'

"The prince replied, 'May God grant you good health, Tomas!' He mounted his horse and in a brisker tone cried from the saddle, 'Take me where I can rest!' So we began to lead him toward the town hall, past two burned buildings and Monsieur de Vielle's looted home. As the Prince passed that house, he asked, 'Is Monsieur de Vielle still alive?'

"Tomas, who was leading the prince's horse by the bridle, replied manfully, 'Monsieur de Vielle is no longer alive; he fell victim to the great anger of Arras.' The prince nodded and grew sad. He asked no more questions."

This is what I was told by Pierre de Moyes, who took part in the council that night.

In the name of the Father, and of the Son, and of the Holy Ghost. Amen. Gentlemen, imagine the thoughts of the people who had waited by Trinity Gate as they conducted the prince to the town hall. No doubt as soon as word had arrived that David was nearing Arras, they realized that nothing could save them. In other words, they assumed responsibility for all the diabolic events that had taken place here.

When a person does evil or good, he can be guided by God's grace or Satan's temptations. But when the hour comes for him to pay for his acts, he is left all alone, abandoned by Heaven and Hell. And thus did the council of the town of Arras walk from the town hall to Trinity Gate, bearing the weight of all the crimes on their shoulders. And no one took fright; no one begged for mercy; nor did anyone deny what had happened. And, of course, they could have, they could have! If they had appealed to their faith during those cruel days, they could have done the same in the presence of Prince David without detriment to themselves. And yet they did not. Clearly, they had lost all faith and, there at the brink, had realized that their God and the devil were both deriding them, making them the laughingstock of the world. For many days and nights they had held up the shield of Providence, confident that it would protect them against everything; but when that shield proved an ordinary dishrag soaked with innocent blood, they threw it away to face the future alone.

What of it that they were guilty, if that guilt had cost them so much despair and isolation? They could undergo no punishment greater than having been deceived by the ostensible destiny to which they had yielded in good faith. They stood by the Trinity Gate so bereft and injured that they no longer had the will to humbly confess their guilt. I even think they did not feel guilty in the way an outsider might expect: they did not feel guilty about what they had done but rather about the good faith in which they had acted. In honest dialogue with themselves, they would not have asked, "Why did you kill innocent people?" but,

"Why did you believe that you should kill people in Arras?" It was no longer important to them whether or not that unfortunate Jew Tselus had cursed the house of the Damascene but only whether or not Tselus should have been dealt with so cruelly.

Oh, gentlemen, the people of the council were never as courageous and splendid as they were that night when Trinity Gate was opened, and David came riding into Arras. Though they had yet to realize what a terrible punishment lay in store for them.

They had been expecting that punishment for a long time and had racked their brains over what form it would take. On the morning after he had ridden in, David announced that on the next Sunday a solemn holy mass would be said, and all sins absolved. So, Arras made ready for the mass, but the council members realized that they would be held accountable later, before the court of the bishopric. Meanwhile, they were free to go about their business although, to tell the truth, there was no sign of them anywhere. They took refuge in their homes, their doors shut tight, each of them very much alone.

But the mass was not said on that next Sunday because Father Albert had given up the ghost the previous day. I have already told you how he died!

Thus, what was to have been a day of joy proved a day of mourning. David ordered a funeral with all pomp and ceremony. And, gentlemen, what would you say about the fact that throngs of people turned out to pay their last respects to Albert? "He's gone now. He erred but he had faith," people said. The

Reverend Father was buried in the Church of the Holy Trinity, in a niche by the great altar. His body had become enormous, and though the weather had turned very cool—there was a light frost at night and some ice on the roofs of the churches—his remains still reeked terribly. Coming apart in places, Albert's body oozed disgusting fluid at every limb. There were some people who said this was the devil seeking to exit the body, but the others paid that no heed. The citizens said, "Albert was a very unfortunate man because he had too much faith." So, he was given solemn burial. There was no love or grief, only that solemnity and a great gathering of the whole town of Arras, which will never be understood by outsiders.

Albert's body was bricked up in a niche by the altar. Masons were much disliked and lived outside the town walls, far from everyone else. They were shaggy men, with long beards, who wore flaxen shorts and went barefoot. But this time, as opposed to usual practice, no one shunned them or crossed themselves when they approached. Some citizens even gave those masons a few coppers, saying, "Do a good job walling him in. He was a poor and very unfortunate man, so let him rest in comfort." When the niche was walled up, the bells rang and the crowd recited a silent prayer.

And so it was on the following Sunday that David said a great mass and announced the annulment of all the trials. And it was on that night that we feasted, and as he drank to my health, that he said that no one was happy. I knew what he meant. Before midnight he had to conduct the trial of the council members. They had been ordered to present themselves in the town hall courtyard. They all came on their own, not under guard.

Finally, Prince David rose and said that we should go with him to the gallery where he would address the town council of Arras, so we left the feast with him. It was a cool and torchlit night. We could hear muffled hubbub from the marketplace, where the common folk had been enjoined to eat, drink, and make merry. The council members were waiting in the town hall courtyard. Pierre de Moyes, Tomas the Lame, and Yvonnet the clothier were there, along with five others, for that was all who remained among the living. I could see their expressions in the glow of the torches placed on gnarled poles around the courtyard.

David looked at them for a long time. His eyes were grave, and I could hear his breath, very shallow, as if a stone lay on his chest. Chastell, who was beside me, whispered, "A bad night, Jan!" I didn't need him to tell me.

Time seemed protracted as it flowed evenly away in the silence of us all. In the town hall, a hush had fallen on the feast, for the feasters wished to hear what David would say to the council. The air swelled only with the breathing of the multitude. There was a light frost, and we were all enveloped in a fine mist. I saw ice flash on top of a tower.

At last the bishop of Utrecht spoke: "How much suffering can the walls of this town contain, and how much can the hearts of its citizens contain? That I do not know, for I am not one of you. And I can only feel great sorrow for the disaster that has befallen my town of Arras. But I do know that disaster arose more out of folly than evilheartedness. What we have here is foolish people, those who are even more foolish, and those most foolish of all! And that means you who sat in session at the council, because you are unable to trust intelligence and trampled on the mind of man. But God sees that this is not the first time this has ever happened in the world. And not the last either. And so I will say but one thing to you! Leave this town forever, and take your womenfolk and children, your cattle and your chattels. May God lead you down the road of reason. And I will say once again what I said to you this day: What happened never happened, and what was, never was! Trust in yourselves, sin in moderation, and pray for the salvation of your souls!"

He made the sign of the cross over all the council and returned to the town hall with a weary tread. The councillors remained where they stood as if thunderstruck.

Hidden in shadow, I watched them for some time. They did not fall to their knees or thank God for being saved in so singular a fashion. They left in complete silence, each by himself, as if they were now divided by all the thoughts and actions that they had once held in common. Each went his own way. I returned to the feast.

It was then that I exploded with such indescribable sorrow, terrible bitterness, and despondency that I felt like screaming and howling with despair for this town, for myself, and for the whole world finally. I sank into my chair beside Prince David and stared at the wall. Chastell spoke to me, but I wasn't listening. Only when the prince took my hand did I whisper softly, "Your Highness, it's all so terrible."

"You are right, Jan," said David. "But we all must reconcile ourselves to the fate we are given. I was beneficent to the council."

"And that's the most terrible thing of all!" said I, interrupting him violently, which I had never done to so great a lord.

"The most terrible thing of all?" said David in surprise. "Something's tangled in your head. I'll tell you: the only terrible thing is the death of a person, not your own death but that of another. Do you know how I have spent my time in the last few weeks while you were drudging away in Arras at Albert's side? I'll tell you. I was called to the bedside of Chevalier Saint Omer, my nephew. Still very young, he was patient in his long dying. In a stuffy room, to the sound of prayers recited by the monk who watched over him day and night. 'Prince,' said that boy, with a face that was innocent and greedy for life, 'I don't want to die yet. Tell God to grant me some time. I'll live an exemplary life and give five ducats for the chapel.' What could I say in answer? That God does not hear prayers like that? I went from the sickroom to the church. I knelt and asked Christ on the Cross to show one drop of mercy. Christ looked at me and kept His silence. Just as always! And I loved that child very much. His ease,

his trust, his humility brought him closer to me than
any others. Poor Saint Omer died, and we buried him
in Ghent as is proper. And I wept then. If you think I
prayed, you are in error. God has not heard my prayers for a long time now, and I too have no wish to
waste time. God and I are at great variance, for I doubt
in Him and He in me. Somehow, He and I manage,
without any great love for each other. When Saint
Omer was dying, I thought, and not for the first time
either, that all this agitation is for naught, that all
entreaties, faith, requests, and blasphemies are for
naught. Our hour comes and it's off we go! There is no
pity for anyone, there never was, and there never will
be. It's not enough that we leave this world; God also
enjoins us to bid farewell to those we love. The very
thought of such cruelty makes my hair stand on end.
First He gives us life and then He steals it back. First,
we are led into temptation, then hurled into darkest
despair. Whatever we touch, dies. And, oh, I'm not
surprised that we seek consolation. It doesn't matter
what, as long as there's something to believe in, to
keep death away from us, to outwit it. When things go
badly for us, we say it's the will of Heaven. When we
act badly, we say it was the way God commanded us
to battle for own salvation. We do not bear each other
gladly and always need something beyond ourselves,
some unhuman force that enlists our hearts and
minds, captivates them, ensnares them, and crushes
them like a boot heel crushes a grain of seed. And
then we think that we have been saved from death,
that now we are free and can live without fear. But

that's all untrue, my dear Jan, for the day comes, the cruelest and solely important day, and then it's off we go! Then everything changes into a dung heap because none of us can stop Death when he comes knocking at our door. Neither God nor the devil is with us anymore, there's nothing but us, just we ourselves, hollowed out by fear, miserable shells, rats, flies, or creatures so small they can't be seen by the eye.

"When young Saint Omer died, I asked myself, where do that child's stars shine now? Why, they are extinguished forever. His stars were different from mine, though they were the same stars. His sun no longer shone, his winds no longer blew about the world, his rain no longer fell on the fields, his trees no longer rustled. Everything vanished, including the God in which he believed, whom he loved and feared. And I remained with my sun, wind, rain, and trees. As for my God, He no longer exists. If I must go off into the darkness, let Him precede me and wait for me there. And maybe He will wait till I arrive there. Why should I poison myself with anticipation, why should I constantly bid farewell to everything that dies before my eyes?

"The Town Council of Arras imagined that as long as they believed fervently in God and in Father Albert's teachings on eternal salvation, peace and freedom would dwell within these walls. Oh, my dear Jan, what was their hurry for joy and happiness? Isn't it better to live a peaceful life, feasting and falconing, and to feel a cool indifference to the world steal into your heart? If you don't greet the day, you need not bid it farewell. If you're not gladdened by the sunrise, you need not be saddened by sunset. If you do not love, you are free from despair. If you do not desire salvation, you do not fear Hell! That's the best of life, isn't it, Jan?! Even if it's attainable, it's only attainable within our own lives and not outside them. The people on the council made a grievous error, but I will not be their judge. I'm feeling too weary to prosecute others for their sins. They've made their beds; let them lie in them. And it wasn't I who led them astray. If I seek the freedom most appropriate for me, I will not deprive them of choice either. Let each man go his own way. The way of the foolish is not for me; but neither shall I attempt to correct them, for it will only come to naught. Let the sober stay with their sobriety, and the madmen with their madness."

As I listened to David, my despair and anger mounted. When he had finished, I cried, "Prince, but you must admit there was something holy about their madness!" David burst out laughing. He laughed so loudly and so long that the others at the table turned and looked intently at us. "Don't laugh, Your Majesty, that's an insult to the memory of all those who went to the block," I said with incredible arrogance.

He replied, his tone now entirely merry, "I forgive you, dear Jan. You must have had too much to drink."

"I'm not drunk, Prince," I said. "But I do know your decision to annul all the trials in Arras was iniquitous. It is not good to say what you said—that what happened never happened, and what was, never was! The truth is that what happened, happened, and what was, was. Your Majesty, you think it's enough to make a sign with your hand to dry all the tears, to wipe away the bloodstains, and for people's consciences to be pure as snow again! But that isn't true! All of us here in Arras have been coated by the gray of sin and now look more like flax than snow, more like black earth than ice. But it's better that way, for a seed may grow out of the earth, but only coldness issues from ice. And you can cover your back with a shirt of flax, but snow gives no cover to a bare arm. Prince, you think you are good and lenient, but you are not! A lack of mercy is as fatal as its excess. And what did you do to the council? You ordered them to leave town, without making any rebuke or punishing anyone, as if nothing whatsoever had happened here. But something did! And though it is your most ardent desire that what was, never was, still it was so. Your Majesty, you are free to dismiss all this, for you are an outsider! But what about us? Is all that vile sin to prove no sin at all, and all that cruelty a trifle? Did the town of Arras slog through the stinking dung of its crimes only to have you now proclaim that not a single step was ever taken? Did we burn people at that stake and torment Jews, commoners, lords, and priests to hear you now say that none of this is true, a blank, the delusion of our poor senses? Do you say that there is no salvation, nothing higher, for the town of Arras and for the whole world? Then, why did son betray father to the council, why were Jewish homes burned, and why were those who called this town heretical torn to pieces? We sank to the depths so as to rise to the heights, and now, Prince, you tell us the effort was in vain! This cannot be in a world created by God. And if created not by God, then by the devil. And if not by the devil, then created by us alone! Your Majesty, have pity on this suffering town that earnestly sought its way, and don't tell us that the only way left to man is to hunt with falcon or feast at table. It can't be. The world would have to collapse, the stars die out, the trees wither. It can't be, it can't be, it can't be. . . ."

In the name of the Father, and of the Son, and of the Holy Ghost. Amen. I wept then as I had never wept before. The tears streamed from my eyes in indescribable sorrow. And the other citizens of Arras at the table wept along with me. Meanwhile, the bishop's court remained silent, quite surprised and taken aback. Everyone was waiting to hear what the bishop of Utrecht would say, for he was known to be my friend. Yet I had insulted him greatly, as no one in Ghent would have dared to. And so all thought that severe punishment lay in store for me. I'll tell you the truth, gentlemen, I thought so too.

David looked at me with an odd expression on his face, one both tender and mocking. "Jan, my dear friend!" he said at last. "I feel sorry for you. And strangest of all is that what I've said here today are things you've professed for many years. Your entire life has been one of reason, and one free of all temptation to seek dreams outside yourself. But you've suffered a great deal lately and were close to a terrible death, and you contemplated fate with more anguish than you'd ever known. . . ." He broke off for a moment and laughed, not without derision. "And I'll tell you what I find most amusing about what you said, but this is only for you to hear." Leaning to my ear, he whispered, so choked with laughter that I had to strain to make him out, "Jan, you scamp! I'm perfectly aware you think and feel the same way I do! And that will never change. The sins you're forgiving here today you'll condemn tomorrow with me! You demand great faith and zeal of heart from the rulers of this world, while allowing others like yourself to mock everything."

"That's not true, Prince," I said softly. By then, my tears had dried up. "You wrong me with such suspicions."

"I know you, you rascal," he replied, still bent to my ear. "You'd like to place all mankind's burdens on the ruler's shoulders, so you can go your merry way. You'll say that's why we have rulers, to save us all and make us better. You sat on the council yourself, and so you know what can be expected of rulers! You demand of them not only holy conviction, but fervent hearts while you would remain cool here today. Oh, but you're a slyboots, Jan! Come to Ghent and be my jester!"

Then I rose from the table, though no one had ever before dared do this in David's presence without his permission. After rising, I said, "I should not hear such words from Your Majesty's lips. Since you condemn the town of Arras to a penance of oblivion, allow me to leave here just as the council has already left."

In reply, David shouted, "Go to Hell, you bore me."

I left the banquet hall and went home. I spent the rest of the night getting ready to travel, and the autumn dawn found me by the wagons that my servants were loading with all my worldly goods.

Chastell appeared at my door at sunrise and announced, "I've come from David to tell you that the bishop forgives everything that happened at the feast. Remain in Arras if you wish, and if you desire to take up residence in Ghent or Utrecht, you will be welcomed as an old friend."

I replied to Chastell, "My dearest friend, tell the bishop that I respect and love him greatly, but I have decided to leave the lands of Burgundy forever. I swear, I don't know why I'm doing this, but it's certainly what I shall do."

Then Chastell embraced me and bid me farewell. Stepping back, he gave me a ring from the bishop and said, "Prince David sent this to you in the event you had decided to leave forever. And he also told me to tell you that even if you do leave, all hope is still not lost for you!" And with that he left.

I went outside to the front of the house to see if the wagons were loaded and ready.

I rode out of Arras through Saint Aegidus' Gate, the same one through which I had walked when entering the town for the first time. It was close to freezing, and clouds of vapor burst from the horses' nostrils. The wagons creaked along, the shouts of my drivers carrying far in the air. I had left a trusted servant in Arras to liquidate my affairs. When he asked where I was going, I didn't know what to tell him.

Outside the walls I dismounted and bowed low to the town of Arras.

Gentlemen, that was a town neither good nor wise, because of what it had suffered. A grievous fate was sent down upon it, and that was why Arras had sinned. Wisdom never goes hand in hand with affliction.

And so I left Arras, letting chance choose my direction. I told myself I'd follow the wind. But the world played yet another trick on me; for when I turned south, the wind suddenly changed direction and now blew straight into my face. Thus, I ordered the wagons turned north. And when the wagons were turned, I said to myself, "You fool! Don't be the plaything of crosswinds." It was then I decided to go to Bruges, a judicious and independent city. Once again the drivers lashed their whips, and the horses pulled the wagons along the ruts in the frozen ground. Riding a charger of good blood, I looked back at the town of Arras vanishing into the distance. I found it strange that it was now I was leaving. Why hadn't I left Arras when Tselus was tried, why only today? I asked myself, somewhat confounded. Why didn't I revolt against Albert and his council when they were seized with holy madness, and why today do I revolt against the bishop, whose discernment I have esteemed my whole life?

I spurred the flanks of my horse, which broke into a gallop, its hooves kicking up clumps of frozen earth. The wind was blowing in my face. I could hear the drivers shouting as they tried to keep up. I gave the horse his head to carry me as fast as possible from that town, and as far away.

In the name of the Father, and of the Son, and of the Holy Ghost. Amen. By then, gentlemen, I knew what I was doing. At some time everyone feels the need to make a great revolt, but one must choose the right hour. Had I left Arras during the madness, I would have saved only my reason, something I never lacked anyway. By leaving after everything was over, however, I saved a scrap of my faith. Not a lot, but enough to live a while longer in this best of worlds.

And by that I mean the glorious city of Bruges and all its citizens. . . .

Warsaw, September 1968–November 1970